Hot SEAL

in

Hollywood

HOT SEALS

Cat Johnson

CHAPTER ONE

"That's it. Good. Gaze deeply into each other's eyes. Hold that. Hold it. And . . . now . . . kiss the girl!"

Scowling, Rick Mann watched the scene unfold in front of him.

The dark haired man, who could have stepped into the leading man's role in any film made between the nineteen-fifties and today thanks to his chiseled classic good looks, leaned in.

The director nodded with approval as his star did as told and kissed the girl. The only problem was, she was Rick's girl.

The one he'd been dating . . .

The one he'd been unofficially living with . . .

The one he'd been in love with . . . for over two

damn years.

As her head of security, Rick had watched Academy Award winning actress Sierra Cox kiss many men, over and over again, through dozens of takes and hours worth of filming.

As her boyfriend, he'd hated every second of it. It was enough to give any man an ulcer.

It had proven enough to make Rick Mann beat the shit out of the punching bag at the local gym nightly—when he could find one.

When he couldn't find a nearby gym with a punching bag, he'd run. Run until his lungs and his legs gave out and his brain had enough endorphins pumping to it that Rick was no longer tempted to beat the crap out of Sierra's co-star instead of a punching bag.

The director said something else Rick missed as the red haze of rage clouded his senses. In response, the couple tumbled onto the mattress.

It didn't matter that the bed was a prop set up in a studio and surrounded by a dozen members of the crew. It was still a bed and they were still naked together in it.

Drawing in a deep breath through his nose, Rick watched, arms crossed, fists tight, blood pressure rising.

"Jamey, I can see the sock," the director said.

The sock. Or more specifically, the *cock sock.* The only mother-fucking piece of clothing—if you could even call it that—separating this naked man's junk from the part of Sierra's body that belonged exclusively to Rick.

Jamey Garret, Hollywood's newest hot leading man, adjusted his naked ass on top of Sierra's equally nude body as Rick's heart pounded.

"Christ." Jaw set, Rick blew out a curse beneath his breath.

The assistant director standing next to him shot him a glare.

Rick knew to be silent once the director shouted action. He wasn't stupid. But he was livid.

The gym wasn't going to do it tonight. He needed to search online for a shooting range. Maybe blowing a few hundred holes in some paper targets would help.

Maybe he could get his hands on one of Jamey's headshots for inspiration.

Shit. What the hell had happened to the cool, calm Navy SEAL he'd been just a few years ago?

Based on his current thoughts, he sounded more like one of the terrorists he'd dedicated half of his adult years to fighting rather than a highly trained operator.

Actually, his inner dialogue sounded like that of a maniacal murderer because it wasn't democracy or masses of innocent civilians he wanted to destroy like the radical jihadists. Oh, no. Rick's crosshairs sat squarely on just one target. A single pretty boy movie star.

Particularly right now because, dammit, this guy was cupping Sierra's naked breasts.

And fuck, now his mouth was on her, sucking

the same nipple Rick had just hours ago.

He'd woken before dawn and, knowing which scene they'd be shooting today, had given Sierra something to remember him by before they left for the lot.

It took some doing, but he'd restrained himself from sucking on her until he bruised her porcelain skin, marking her as his territory like some wild animal.

Even with as wild as he felt watching this shit happening in front of him, the logical part of his brain knew she'd be pissed and embarrassed if the make-up people had to cover her hickeys because her boyfriend couldn't handle seeing her make out with her hunky co-star.

Meanwhile, the bastard had graduated from just kissing Rick's girl, to making love to her.

Okay, so it was simulated movie sex, but it felt all too real as Rick watched.

It looked pretty frigging real too as Jamey thrust his hips against Sierra, who reacted by scratching her nails down his back.

Fuck. Rick had experienced how that felt first hand. If this man wasn't hard enough to drive nails by now, he must be gay.

Gay. That would be perfect. Rick could definitely handle that. Feeling hopeful for the first time since this production began, Rick grasped on to the possibility.

Hell, he and Jamey might even become good friends. Rick could use a guy friend out here. He'd spent so much time in California lately he'd been sorely missing his buddies back on the east coast.

His assumption on Jamey's sexuality firmly in place, Rick watched the scene with a new calm, finally able to appreciate some of the Hollywood magic. How glaring lights and hundreds of hours of raw footage could be edited down, cut together and set to music to become two hours of seamless entertainment the public willingly shelled out millions of dollars collectively to enjoy.

It really was quite a production. As complicated as any mission he'd been on in the teams, though far less deadly.

In Hollywood, death meant not killing it in box office returns opening weekend.

He'd spent a decade in the SEALs dealing with a more definitive kind of killing and death.

"And cut! All right. Let's take five. Good job, everybody." The director's words caught Rick's attention.

He dragged himself out of the haze he'd been in and focused on the action in front of him.

People scrambled everywhere, including the young woman who ran toward Sierra carrying a white robe.

Thank God for that. If Rick had to watch his woman be naked in front of Mr. Box Office for one more minute, he was going to lose his shit.

Christ. He'd already lost it. He should be sweeping the perimeter, making sure no one was being allowed on set who shouldn't be here. He should be watching every person on the set, making sure he knew them all and their purpose for being here.

Hell, he should just demand they have a closed set, especially for scenes like this.

Although maybe not . . . Then Sierra rolling around naked in bed with Mr. Sex on Sheets would seem even more intimate.

At least now, surrounded by the circus that was movie making, Rick—and more importantly, Jamey—would be reminded this wasn't real.

But shit, it sure felt real.

And fuck, as Jamey turned sideways to pull on his own robe, his full-tilt bobbing erection horizontally straining the confines of the cock sock was clearly visible . . . and Rick was back to feeling like he had to puke.

Not gay.

Rick reached into his pocket for his roll of antacids. He'd started to buy large economy packs of this shit since one roll barely lasted him until lunch.

He'd survived a decade in the teams, in hell holes and war zones world wide, but this movie might just kill him.

Meanwhile, Sierra was happy as a clam in this environment. Show business was in her blood and she was completely in her element here.

She loved LA as much as Rick hated it. Her striding toward him now with a huge smile on her face was proof of that.

Shit. It was looking more and more as if she was going to want to move out here. He missed Virginia. Missed his teammates. Even missed his annoying sister.

At least Sierra's house in Miami was on the east coast, close enough he could travel home to Virginia as often as he wanted. But California . . . right now it felt like the other side of the world.

"Hey. What's wrong?" Sierra asked, her perfectly shaped brows low.

"Hmm?" Rick dragged his attention away from the *poor me* thoughts running on a continuous loop in his head.

He redirected his focus to the cause of it—his beautiful girlfriend, who might not be his girl for much longer if she decided she liked her pretty boy co-star better.

Carey Jones had been Rick's whole universe for over two years—but the rest of the world only knew her as actress Sierra Cox and him as her bodyguard.

It had felt safer that way—smarter back when they'd started dating—to keep him anonymous and in the shadows where he was most comfortable anyway.

Now it just felt like he was her sidepiece. A dirty little secret. The unknown and unimportant bodyguard who had no claim on her and no recourse except to silently watch as men thought she was available.

Jaw set, he drew in a breath. "Sorry. What did you say?"

7

Sierra frowned, evaluating him. "I asked if something was wrong. You look all . . . scary."

He laughed at that. Scary? Shit. She knew he would never hurt her.

Her co-star on the other hand . . .

"Did something happen?" She glanced around them. "Did you see someone who shouldn't be here?"

At least now, for once, she was taking his warnings about her crazy fans and potential stalkers seriously. When they'd first met, she hadn't listened to his advice on her safety until someone had actually taken a shot at them.

This was progress. Two years late, but progress none-the-less. But no, he hadn't seen anything or anyone because he'd been too fucking worried about where her co-star's dick was lodged as he rolled on top of her.

Rick drew in a breath. "I'm just . . . distracted."

Speaking of distractions—Jamey walked up to them, smiling like he'd just been skin-to-skin with one of the hottest women in Hollywood.

Oh, wait. That's exactly where he'd been. Rick felt his fists clench.

"Hey." Jamey directed a quick glance at Rick before focusing on Sierra. "How do you think this scene is going?" he asked her.

"Fine. Don't you think so?" she asked, looking way more concerned about poor Jamey's feelings than she had about Rick's mood before.

Jamey lifted one shoulder beneath the white

robe. "I don't know. I'm not sure it feels . . . real. You know?"

A snort he couldn't control escaped Rick, earning him a questioning look from both Sierra and Jamey.

Hell, at least they'd remembered he was there.

"Sorry." He ran his hand across his mouth and pretended he didn't want to throttle the guy. How good would it feel to knock him and his monogrammed bathrobe right on his terrycloth-covered ass?

Sierra looked back to the pretty boy. "You have to realize, it's not going to feel real during the shooting with all this around us . . ." She waved a hand to indicate the chaos surrounding them.

"Feels fucking real enough to me," Rick mumbled.

As she shot him another glare, he pressed his lips together in an attempt to keep silent.

"I'm not talking about the sex. I meant more the emotions. The words. I don't know." Jamey shook his head. "I'm just not buying it. Staring into each other's eyes for like five minutes after an hour's worth of build-up on screen . . . that's not how it would go. In real life, he'd be all over her."

It had looked like Jamey had been all over her, just like Rick had been the first time he and Sierra had fallen into bed together. But the kid was right. There'd been no eye gazing involved for the two of them back then. Even so, there was no way Rick was going to side with this dickhead on the issue.

Sierra lifted a shoulder. "It's cinema. Things are drawn out for dramatic effect."

"I guess." He sighed.

"Would it help if we ran the scene a few different ways, maybe off camera without the director?" Sierra suggested.

Oh sure. Rick was certain pretty boy would just love that. Another huff of air escaped him.

Sierra narrowed her eyes at Rick. She opened her mouth when the shout came for them to get back to their places.

She shot Rick one more glare and turned to Jamey. "Come on. We'll talk about this later."

Jamey nodded and laid one hand on her lower back as she led the way back to the big bed.

With his focus zeroed in on that hand touching her, Rick mouthed a string of silent cusses as his pulse pounded in his ears.

He heard a laugh next to him and looked over to see one of the lighting crew. "Dude, you should just go. Do something else. It's only going to get worse."

"What do you mean?"

"They're just getting started. This scene could take all day." He shook his head. "You probably don't want to be here to see it."

Maybe their relationship wasn't all that discreet after all. Good. At least one person on set knew Sierra belonged to Rick and could appreciate what he was going through.

"I can't leave," Rick said.

"Why not? What's gonna happen? She's on camera and the doors are locked once they yell *action*. She's safe. Jamey, on the other hand." The guy cocked up a brow. "You look about ready to murder him."

Rick closed his eyes for a second, centering himself. "It's that obvious?" he asked, bringing his gaze to the guy next to him.

"Oh yeah."

He drew in a breath. Leaving—at least for a little while—might save his sanity. "How long you think this shit's going to go for?" he asked.

"That depends on a lot of things. Some nights we're here until one in the morning."

Great. Rick should be good and insane by then. But there was no way he was going back to the hotel and waiting there until the middle of the night for Sierra to come home. He could, however, take his surveillance outdoors for a bit.

A little fresh air and sunshine could help his disposition.

He might as well take advantage of the perfect California weather. He hated everything else about this place but he had to admit the weather was a check in the *pro* column. The only check.

"All right. I'm gonna be outside—"

"And action!"

That call had Rick mouthing another curse as the guy next to him laughed silently.

The doors were locked. He wasn't getting outside anytime soon. At least not until they called

11

cut.

His gaze hit upon the scene on the bed one more time.

He reached for another antacid.

CHAPTER TWO

Sierra had to catch the suite's door to keep it from swinging shut on her as Rick stalked inside ahead of her.

It was the end of a really long day that had begun at five a.m. in the makeup chair and hadn't ended until well after sunset and thirty takes of a sex scene that should have been a piece of cake but for some reason, wasn't proving so.

That didn't stop Rick from having plenty of energy to stride across the living area and directly into the bedroom like a man on a mission.

Standing in the bedroom doorway, she watched as he moved toward the dresser while stripping.

He dropped his clothes in a pile on the floor. After pulling out a pair of shorts from the drawer, he sat on the edge of the bed and tugged them up his thick thighs.

She knew what that meant. He was going to the hotel gym or for a run. Somewhere, anywhere, as long as it was away from her, or so it seemed.

It had become his habit since filming had begun.

When he grabbed a T-shirt and a pair of socks and turned toward the doorway, she stood her ground, blocking his way out of the bedroom.

"What was wrong with you today?" Sierra planted her hands on her hips and faced the man head on.

He might be taller, wider, heavier, but she was angrier.

"Nothing's wrong." He had the decency to drop his gaze to the carpet and look contrite.

"You know what my job entails. Why were you stomping around like a Neanderthal in front of Jamey today? I half expected you to grab me by the hair and drag me out of there and back to your cave—"

He held up one hand, palm facing her. "All right. Enough with the caveman analogy. I get it. I behaved badly."

Still pissed off by his rude behavior on set, Sierra said, "Ooo, *analogy*. That's a big word. Didn't know you knew any four-syllable words."

The expression on his face—shock mixed with hurt—had her immediately regretting her words.

His nostrils flared as he physically moved her out of the way and took a step into the living room.

"Rick. Wait." She jumped to follow him, reached out and grabbed his arm. He stopped walking, but didn't turn around. "I'm sorry. I didn't mean it. I'm just frustrated."

She watched his broad back seem to expand and contract as he drew in a big breath and let it out. Finally, he turned to look at her. "There's truth behind every joke. You know that."

He'd said that to her before. She didn't believe it then. She didn't want to believe it now. She shook her head. "No—"

"Yes," he interrupted her. "You think I'm stupid. I didn't go to college. I'm not famous. I'm not rich. You think I'm not good enough for you."

"No, I don't." She took a step forward and laid her hands on the bare skin of his broad hard chest. She felt the dusting of course hair growing there tickle her palms.

He turned his head, refusing to look at her, choosing instead to focus on the wall behind her. He didn't touch her but she could feel his heart thundering beneath her hands.

She'd hurt him but she hadn't meant to. She just wanted him to stop acting like an idiot on set.

There was no excuse for his jealousy. She might pretend to have sex on camera with other men, but he was the one she came home to every night. The only one she wanted to go to bed with for real.

After being with her for over two years, he should be used to this life. Obviously, he wasn't.

Yes, this particular movie was hotter than her

usual, but Rick needed to get over it. This script had Oscar nomination written all over it and Jamey was a huge new name on the scene that might just revive a career that she was beginning to fear was nearing its sunset years.

Women didn't age well in Hollywood. If doing a couple of sex scenes with a hot young star like Jamey would buy her a few more years at the top of the box office, then she was going to do it.

Rick needed to understand that. Still, her insulting his intelligence wasn't going to help the situation.

"I'm sorry," she said.

"Sorry you said it? Or sorry you mean it?" he asked, hurt and anger making his voice deeper, raspier, than usual.

That voice, low and sensual against her ear in bed, had always gotten to her. She loved it then, when it was caused by passion. She didn't enjoy it now. It was one more reminder how deeply she'd cut him with her words.

"Rick, I say things I don't mean all day long—"

He pinned her with his gaze. "When you're with me it's supposed to be different. We're supposed to be real."

"We are real." She pressed closer to his body.

He breathed in again, his chest expanding against her, but still he didn't touch her or hold her, just when she really needed him to.

"I didn't mean it. I'm so sorry I said it." Raising on tip-toe in her high heels she pressed a kiss to his chin, then to the corner of his mouth.

His gaze dropped to hers as she moved and brushed her lips against his.

"I'm so sorry," she repeated, before taking the kiss deeper.

Finally, he tossed the T-shirt and socks he'd had clenched in one fist onto the chair nearby.

He raised his hands and rested them on her arms, but for a second she wasn't sure if it was to pull her closer or push her away. Then he was kissing her back.

Rick took possession of her mouth with a passion that reminded her of the days when they'd first met. Back when they'd argue themselves into a frenzy and work off the anger in bed.

Was that what this was for him? Anger-fueled hate-sex?

As much as she didn't want to believe that, she'd take it, because any contact with him was preferable to being frozen out.

He ran his hands down to cup her ass and haul her up until her feet left the ground.

She wrapped her legs around his waist as he carried her to the bedroom.

He tossed her onto the bed and followed her down, his bulk pressing her into the mattress. She loved the weight of him on top of her. It made her feel safe, taken, wanted.

While his head was buried against her neck, he shoved the waistband of his shorts down and the skirt of her dress up.

Maybe Jamey was right when he'd said their sex scene today felt fake. Here, now, with Rick, there were no long soulful glances. No slow tender touches. Just raw need.

That was the last work-related notion she had as thick fingers pushed her underwear aside and Rick sought and found his end goal. He worked her fast and hard with his hand before he reached down and lined up his length with her entrance.

He plunged deep inside, driving the breath from her lungs and all rational thought from her head.

Hooking one hand behind her knee, he lifted her leg and opened her to him, taking her deeper.

She watched the raw emotion on his face as, with his eyes slammed tightly closed, he loved her hard and fast. She watched until he opened his eyes and saw her watching.

His gaze narrowed as he changed position, rising onto his knees as he lifted her bottom and shoved a pillow beneath her.

He knew exactly what he was doing. The new angle made it so his every thrust hit her G-spot until she couldn't hold her eyes open any longer.

Throwing her head back against the pillow, she clutched at his forearms as she gasped. He waited for her to come and followed immediately after, matching her spasms with his strokes until, spent, he collapsed on top of her.

"I love you," she said, her words muffled against his chest.

"Do you?" he asked, lifting up and rolling his

weight off her and onto his side.

She frowned. "You know I do."

He closed his eyes briefly, before opening them again on an exhale. Where there had been anger before, there was now a turmoil of emotions. If she weren't mistaken, shame among them.

"I know. I just can't take it. I thought I could but, Sierra, it's so hard." He blew out a bitter laugh. "We spend so much time in public, I don't even think of you as Carey anymore. It's like our whole life together is fake."

She pinned him with her gaze. "This—you and me—that's not fake."

"On set it sure feels that way. I think a total of one guy knows we're together. Everyone else just thinks I'm your bodyguard."

"You want to come out as a couple? Fine. We'll do it. I'll get my publicist on it, if that's what you want. But trust me when I tell you, you're not going to like it."

He lifted a shoulder. "Maybe I will."

"No *maybe* about it, Rick. I know you. All it's going to take is the paparazzi getting in your face, hounding you while you're running or working out or going to the store or whatever and you're going to regret ever linking your name with mine romantically in public."

"I'd never regret that."

She saw the hurt and doubt in his eyes again. "I'm not trying to hide you. I'm trying to protect you."

"I'm a big boy. And it's my job to protect you, not the other way around."

"You might have been a SEAL, but you're swimming with the sharks now, Rick."

His lips twitched. "How long you been waiting to use that line?" he asked.

The mood had lifted a bit. She could feel it and she grabbed on to the ray of light. "I just thought of it. Pretty good, huh?"

"Eh, it was all right." He tried and failed to control a hint of a crooked smile.

She brushed a hand over the corner of his mouth and cupped his cheek. "I love you. I want to be with you. And I'll only ever come home to you."

He watched her for a second, as if evaluating the truth in her words. "I love you too. I'm sorry I've been a dick. But seriously, that fucking cock sock—"

She laughed. She couldn't help it. He frowned, glaring at her.

"I'm sorry, but hearing the words *cock sock* coming out of your mouth, I couldn't help myself."

"Yeah, well I'm not going to be able to control myself if I have to keep seeing it." He snorted out a breath. "But I'll try my best."

"That's all I can ask. The only easy day was yesterday, you know." She proudly quoted the words printed on one of his T-shirts, but it only earned her a frown.

"That's not helpful," he said, pulling his mouth to the side unhappily.

"I don't get points for my Navy SEAL knowledge?" She put on a pretend pout.

"No. But you might get some sushi take-out since I'm starving and willing to go out and get it for us."

"They will deliver, you know."

"And take an extra hour to do it, and then the hot food will be getting cold and the cold food will be getting warm." He shook his head. "Nope. I'll go out for it. You can stay here."

That was a good plan since she needed a post-coital shower. On top of that, she had some work to do before tomorrow's scenes.

"Okay. I can read over the new pages for tomorrow. Shit." She huffed out an annoyed breath when she remembered the last place she'd been looking over those pages.

"What?" he asked.

"I left them in my trailer." She'd been so flustered by Rick's continued disappearances from the set today, and his storming around looking angry during the times that he was there, it was no surprise she'd been scattered. "I guess I could study the pages in the makeup chair tomorrow morning—"

"No. It's fine. I'll call in the order, run by the lot, and by the time I grab your pages, the food should be ready."

"You are so organized. Must be that military training." She smiled.

He rolled his eyes. "Is this your attempt at

flattery?"

"Maybe. Is it working to cheer you up?"

"That little white lace nighty of yours will work better," he said.

"Duly noted." She nodded and delivered a salute in an attempt to make him laugh again.

She wasn't disappointed. Rick shook his head but smiled as he pulled on his shorts again.

"The usual order for you?" he asked as he bent to retrieve his sneakers from the floor of the closet.

"Yup."

"All right. I'll be back in a bit." He leaned over her on the bed and pressed a kiss to her mouth.

She watched him walk through the door and into the living room, enjoying the view of his back muscles until he pulled on his T-shirt.

Maybe she shouldn't get annoyed that he spent so much time at the gym after all.

CHAPTER THREE

Rick liked the movie lot a hell of a lot better when it was deserted.

Tonight, all he'd seen so far were the guard at the gate and a couple of maintenance guys.

Perfect. If only it could be like this all the time. Quiet. Peaceful.

"Yeah, I know. She's sweet, right?" The sound of Jamey's voice coming from around the other side of the trailer stopped Rick dead in his tracks.

Not so peaceful after all.

Apparently he wasn't the only one who'd come back to the lot after hours. He stopped walking and pressed closer to the trailer, inching his way toward the corner so he could hear better.

Rick used all of his stealth SEAL skills . . . to

eavesdrop on his girlfriend's co-star.

He wasn't as ashamed about that as he probably should be, although it wasn't lost on him how much his life—and his focus—had altered radically since being medically retired from the teams.

His abilities used to be employed in life and death situations.

As he hid in the shadows, waiting for Jamey to say more, Rick couldn't ignore exactly how much his blown out knee had changed his future. It was about as much as meeting Sierra had changed his world.

"No, not yet," Jamey said. "But she's gonna be mine. I promise you that. I'll do whatever the fuck I have to to get her."

The red haze of uncontrolled rage clouded Rick's brain.

Fists clenched as tightly as his jaw, he took another step forward, not caring that it put him in view of the man he'd been avoiding being seen by.

"Yeah. I'm gonna see if I can get her away from her owner tonight. Take her out for another spin."

Rick dragged in a breath as he started to shake.

Another spin. What the fuck?

Was Sierra cheating on him, and with this son of a bitch who'd just admitted she belonged to someone else? To Rick?

There was no controlling himself.

Fist clenched, Rick strode forward, reared back and swung as hard as he could, throwing all six-feet-two-inches and two-hundred pounds of solid muscle behind the punch.

It was enough to send the cell phone flying out of Jamey's hand before it spun the man around and sent him sprawling face down on the ground.

He flopped onto his back, touching the side of his face where Rick's punch had possibly broken his cheekbone. Though that wasn't easy to see through the blood gushing from the cut the punch had also caused.

Jamey looked completely stunned, as if unable to comprehend what had happened or who'd done it.

Panting and shaking with the adrenaline that still pumped through his veins, Rick loomed over the man on the ground. He had no problem letting Jamey know exactly who had put him there and why.

Finally, Jamey looked like he could focus his eyes and his rattled brain on Rick. "Jesus. What was that for?"

Rick clenched his fist again and felt the numbness beginning to be replaced with pain.

Throbbing, intense pain.

He'd punched this guy so hard, he'd be lucky if he hadn't broken his hand.

Fuck it. It had been worth it.

Besides, somewhere in the back of his brain—the part that could still reason through the anger—Rick realized the pain of broken bones would be nothing compared to the pain of Sierra cheating on him.

Once he let that fully settle in—once the anger and adrenaline fled—there'd be nothing but heartache. And he wouldn't even be able to punch his way out of it at the gym thanks to this bastard's face breaking his hand.

That made him even madder. Jaw clenched, he said, "That's for fucking my girlfriend."

Jamey shook his head, still looking dazed. "What are talking about?"

"Sierra."

The guy's one eye widened as the other started to swell shut. "You're her boyfriend? I just thought you were just her bodyguard."

"Yeah, well, I'm not just her bodyguard." Rick moved in closer and Jamey held up his hands in a defensive move.

"All right. All right. It doesn't matter anyway, because I'm not having sex with her. What we do on set, that's all fake. You do know that, right?" Jamey struggled to sit up, and settled for bracing himself on one elbow while still lying on the ground and once again fingering his face.

"She's sweet. I'm gonna make her mine. I don't care about her owner. I'm taking her out for another spin tonight." Rick mimicked the pretty boy in the most unflattering voice he could muster before glaring at him once again and allowing his own baritone to return. "Sound familiar, asshole?"

Jamey's mouth dropped open. "That's what this is about? My phone conversation?"

"Yeah, dickhead. It's about your bragging about

fucking Sierra." The rage began to return as images of them rolling around naked had Rick seeing red.

He stepped forward, which had him standing over the guy, straddling him, which is when Jamey had the nerve to let out a laugh.

How stupid could a man be?

"Oh, I wouldn't be laughing if I were you." Rick bent, about to haul him up by his overpriced shirt so he could knock him down again, when Jamey shook his head.

"Dude. I was talking about a bike."

With a handful of Jamey's T-shirt twisted in his left fist, Rick frowned. "What?"

"I'm buying a vintage motorcycle. The owner's being a dick and playing hardball about the price. I was going to drive over tonight, take it for another ride and see if he'll come down on the price."

Shit. Rick released his hold and took a step back.

Jamey gingerly touched his cheek. "I guess I'll be going to the ER instead."

The regret, along with the dread of what kind of fallout he'd just brought down on himself, made Rick feel almost as bad as when he'd thought Sierra had cheated on him.

Jamey hissed in a breath and dropped his hand from his face. "It's bad, isn't it?"

His regret didn't instill any pity in Rick. Had the pretty boy never gotten punched before? *Big baby*.

"It ain't pretty," Rick told him, not sugar coating the words.

"The director is gonna freak. This could stall production. The continuity is going to be fucked if make-up can't hide this shit."

The movie. Shit. Rick had momentarily forgotten about that, but pretty boy was right. Delays cost extra money and that made the producers insane.

Rick evaluated pretty boy's cheek again. It was rapidly blowing up.

Yeah, make-up wasn't going to cover that. The black eye and bruising that would probably come next—maybe—but not that swelling. And he'd probably need a couple of stitches for the cut. The blood was already beginning to soak Jamey's shirt.

Angry—at himself for losing control and at pretty boy for making him—Rick knew he had to make this right.

He reached down a hand to Jamey. "Come on. I'll drive you to the hospital."

After a few seconds, Jamey took the offered help and Rick hauled him upright.

Rick glanced around and spotted Jamey's cell phone where it had landed about ten feet away. He picked it up and held his breath, hoping it wasn't cracked since it was probably one of those new ones that cost as much as most people's rent for the month.

Luckily it was in a sturdy case. He handed it to Jamey, who took it with a grunt of thanks before shoving it into his pocket with the hand that wasn't trying to stop the flow of blood.

Rick had a napkin in his pocket from lunch, when he'd managed to choke down some foo-foo veggie wrap in between antacids and sex scenes.

He thrust it at Jamey. "Here, hold this on that cut. It's not clotting."

Jamey pressed the napkin to his cheek. "No surprise. Face wounds always bleed like a mother fucker."

Rick let out a snort. Even though what Jamey had said was the truth, he seriously doubted this guy had any first hand experience in wounds of any variety. Maybe paper cuts from opening his royalty checks.

"Had a lot of face wounds, have you?" Rick asked, not hiding the sarcasm in his tone.

Jamey shot him a sideways glance as they began to walk. "A few."

"Plastic surgery?" Rick suggested, feeling petty.

Jamey swiveled his head to look at Rick full on. "You really hate me, don't you?"

Rick opened his mouth, then shut it again, not sure what to say. Finally, he opted on saying nothing.

Shaking his head, Jamey continued, "No, not plastic surgery. I grew up in the foster care system. I was ten the first time my cheekbone was broken. I was eighteen the second time. At least I won money during that fight. Though most of it went to the doctor. So, sorry to tell you, but you don't get the honor of being the first one to make me bleed or send me to the ER."

Rick stopped. After another step, Jamey paused as well and turned back, the question of what the hold up was clear in his expression.

"I'm sorry," Rick said.

Jamey's mouth tipped up in one corner. "It's okay. I understand. I'd lose my fucking mind if I had to watch my girl with another guy all damn day too."

"Yeah, it sucks. Believe me. But I should have been able to handle it." Rick ran a hand over his face. "And you're right. Thanks to me the movie is fucked. I'm definitely fucked. I'll be lucky if Sierra doesn't break up with me. I'll definitely be thrown off set."

Jamey shook his head. "Nah. I'll cover for you."

Rick frowned. "What do you mean?"

"I mean I'll just say I got into a bar fight or something so you don't get into trouble."

Crap. Why the fuck did this guy have to be so nice? Just when Rick was happily hating him, he not only turned out to be a normal guy who'd survived what sounded like a horribly tough upbringing, he was also decent.

Hell, way more than just decent. Jamey was willing to take the fall for Rick's mistake.

He couldn't allow that. Rick shook his head. "No. Thanks, but I did it. I'll take responsibility for it."

Jamey pressed his lips tight. "You sure? Because I think you're right. You'll probably be thrown off set for good and there's like two months left."

"I'm aware." Sixty-nine days on the schedule to be exact. Rick had been crossing them off one by one in an effort to keep his sanity. As it turns out, obsessing over this movie might have only made him crazier. "But the fact remains, I've got to take responsibility for my actions."

"All right. I respect that. I think you're nuts but I respect it."

Rick laughed. "Better they throw me off set than you. The studio wouldn't be happy with you if they thought you'd gone out in the middle of production, got in a bar fight and messed up your pretty face in the process."

Jamey lifted one shoulder. "Eh, the publicist would just spin it. Work the bad boy angle. Movie goers love that shit."

"But I know producers don't. Especially when it costs them money," Rick said.

Jamey laughed. "You've probably been around more movie sets than me but yeah, even I know that."

"What do you mean?" Rick asked, still feeling like an absolute newbie in this business.

"This is only my second movie. And shooting the first one was nothing like this. It was one of those low budget productions that broke out at Sundance and made it big."

"Really?" Rick hadn't realized that.

He knew this kid was new on the Hollywood scene but he hadn't realized exactly how new or how inexperienced.

"Yeah. I was working at a gym and doing some fighting on the side. Two guys showed up, said they were making a movie and asked if I would be in it. I said sure. They weren't paying that much but hey, cash is cash and to get paid and not have to take any real punches to do it—I was in." He shrugged. "That was it. The movie hit. Suddenly I found myself with an agent and a contract and that's how I got here. Hey, can we pop into my trailer so I can change my shirt?"

That would be better for everyone. They'd attract a little less attention if he didn't bring Hollywood's newest darling into the ER covered in blood.

"Sure." Rick nodded. If only he could erase the rest of the evidence of what he'd done as easily.

Inside Jamey's trailer, Rick found pretty much the same set up that Sierra had in hers. Except, instead of make-up and clothes, this guy had barbells on the floor and a jumbo jug of protein powder on the counter.

Against all odds, Rick's number one enemy was . . . normal. Average even.

As much as he hated it, Rick was starting to really like this guy. Enough so that he was feeling in the mood to confess a few things himself.

As Jamey pulled off the bloody shirt, Rick said, "My path to Hollywood was pretty odd and rambling too. And I'm about as new to it as you are."

"For real?" New shirt in hand, Jamey glanced at

Rick. "I'd never have guessed. You look so . . . comfortable on set."

Maybe he should try his hand at acting because he was far from comfortable in this environment. And being on this set in particular had probably done irreparable damage to his body and mind.

"Yeah, no." Rick laughed. "I retired from the Navy when I blew out my knee. Sierra hired the company my friends run in Virginia to handle her security on a movie she was filming there. I was her bodyguard. Then one thing led to another and here I am. That was a little over two years ago."

"Huh. Seems we're both fish out of water around here then."

"Yeah, that's a good way to put it."

Jamey pressed a towel against his face and pulled it away again. "I think it's clotting."

Rick moved closer and evaluated the wound. "Looks like it did." But it still wasn't pretty.

"Good. I'm not going to bother with stitches then.

Rick frowned. "You don't want to go to the hospital?"

"Nah." Jamey studied his reflection in the mirror. "I've got some butterfly bandages around here somewhere. There's ice in the freezer. That and some Ibuprofen and I'll be good to go."

"Okay. Up to you." Not that it mattered much. Stitches or no stitches, what looked bad now was going to look even worse in the morning.

Jamey turned back to face Rick. "I'd rather have

a drink than sit in a waiting room for the next couple of hours. Want one?"

Rick lifted a brow. "You want to have a drink with me? After what I did to you?"

"Better than drinking alone." Jamey opened a cabinet and pulled out a bottle of bourbon and two glasses. "Unless you need to get back to Sierra."

"I have a bit of time." At this point any delay in his having to go back to the hotel and confess to Sierra what he'd done seemed like a good plan. He'd have to get their take-out food and her pages and get back shortly, but after tonight, a drink definitely seemed in order. "I guess I can have one."

Jamey nodded and splashed the amber liquid into the glasses before carrying one over to Rick.

After pulling out a few pieces of ice from the freezer and wrapping them in the towel, he grabbed his own glass.

"So what did you do in the Navy?" Sprawling on the sofa with a drink in one hand, Jamey held the ice on his cheek with the other.

So they were going to do this? Have a normal conversation, as if Rick hadn't been the one to break his face?

Hell, why not?

"I was in the SEALs," Rick said.

"What? Shit. For real?" Jamey's eyes—or at least the one that wasn't swelling shut—opened wider.

This exact reaction was why Rick didn't tell many people the details about his prior service.

"Yeah." Rick rolled his eyes. "Why? Was it your boyhood dream to be a SEAL or something?"

"No. I wanted to be a race car driver when I was little. But you do know what this movie is about, right?"

Rick lifted a shoulder. "You and Sierra having sex?"

Jamey let out a short laugh. "Besides that. My character was a SEAL. There's a bunch of flashback scenes of when he was still in the Navy."

Rick drew his brows low. "I didn't know that."

Why didn't he know that? Probably because he was so busy obsessing over the sex scenes.

So there was more to this movie than just sex. That was a relief.

"We haven't shot any of those scenes yet so I guess if you didn't read the script you wouldn't know," Jamey said. "There's a scene where I'm supposed to be explaining what Hell Week was like to Sierra. It's pretty intense."

A laugh escaped Rick. "*Intense* is one word for it."

"Can you tell me what that was like?" Jamey leaned forward, forearms on his knees as he sat, eyes wide, and looked eager.

Rick's brows rose. Describe Hell Week accurately to a man who'd never been through it? Who was a civilian, no less? Not a chance.

He decided on the first word that came to mind. "Wet."

"Wet?" Jamey laughed. "That's it?"

Rick considered that. "And cold."

Though that might not be accurate. He hadn't read the script and didn't know what time of year the character was supposed to have gone through Hell Week. The discomfort was constant, but whether you roasted or froze varied with the season.

"And sometimes hot," Rick added, for accuracy. "And sandy. Always sandy."

That was one thing he'd never forget—the sand. In his mouth. In his eyes. Sand that scraped his skin until he had a thousand tiny cuts that felt like they were on fire.

Jamey nodded. "And they starve you guys to make it harder. Right?"

"No." Rick shook his head. "We got fed plenty. They deprived us of sleep to make it harder."

"See! That's what I'm worried about." Jamey threw his hands up and flopped back against the sofa cushion. "They've got me saying that we were literally starved during Hell Week. What else did they get wrong in the script? This is exactly why I was afraid to take this part in the first place."

"Don't they have military consultants for this kind of shit?" Rick asked.

"Supposedly some guy went over the script and helped the costume department with the uniforms, but he wasn't a SEAL."

Rick sighed, thinking about every movie and television show he'd watched that had gotten it all wrong, right down to the uniforms, in spite of having *experts* advising them.

"If it'll make you feel better, I'll take a look at Sierra's script."

"Oh my God. Yes! Would you? Thank you."

"Sure. No problem." After what he'd done to the star of this movie's face, Rick owed the production company a free consultation, at the very least.

It would be interesting if nothing else. He hadn't read any of her scripts. He hadn't wanted to have those sex scenes burnt into his brain with words in addition to having to watch it all play out on set in front of him.

Maybe he could just skip to the military parts. Or offer some tips while on set if he saw something wrong during the actual filming.

If he was still around.

After tonight, he likely wouldn't be spending another day on set.

Shit, he was going to have to arrange for someone else to take over Sierra's security on the lot in his absence.

He couldn't protect her if he wasn't even allowed in the gate. And he knew from first hand experience a movie lot wasn't as safe as they all liked to think. He wasn't about to leave her completely unprotected.

Damn, he'd fucked up. That realization was really starting to settle in. It brought Rick's mood down further than it had been.

He raised his glass to his lips and emptied it, relishing the last of the burn down his throat. It might be the last good thing he enjoyed for the near future.

Standing, he took the couple of steps necessary to cross the width of the trailer. He set down the empty glass with a *clunk* on the counter next to the bottle Jamey had left there.

Fun time was over.

"Time to get back," he said.

Back to Sierra to face the music. He couldn't avoid telling her forever that he'd broken her co-star's face.

He glanced at Jamey one last time and cringed. "I really am sorry." For so many reasons.

Jamey waved away the apology. "Hey, if this is what it took for you to agree to be my personal military consultant on this film, it was well worth it."

Rick laughed, his hand on the doorknob. "I didn't agree to that."

"You will. You'll see." Jamey smiled and then winced, no doubt from the pain in his cheek.

Feeling a new rush of guilt, Rick nodded. "We'll see."

CHAPTER FOUR

Rick swung by Sierra's trailer and found the pages she said she needed easily enough. They were right on the table where she'd left them next to her water bottle.

The take-out order was of course ready and sitting in a brown paper bag on the counter of the restaurant by the time Rick got there.

He'd taken so long—beating the shit out of Jamey and then making nice afterward—the food had probably sat there for half an hour.

He should have let the damn place deliver it, the way Sierra had wanted. It might have saved his job.

It sure as hell would have saved his fist, which was aching now that the pain-numbing surge of adrenaline had completely subsided.

With the bag of takeout held in his left hand, Rick opened his right one wide and flexed his fingers a couple of times.

As he faced the door of Sierra's hotel room, he had a feeling his hand was the least of his worries.

With no reason to delay going inside—except that he plain didn't want to—he slid the keycard into the slot and watched the green light welcome him inside. He could only hope Sierra would welcome him inside again as well after he told her what he'd done.

She was sitting on the sofa when he walked in.

He put the bag on the coffee table in front of her and opened his mouth to begin his apology when he realized she was talking on the phone through the Bluetooth earpiece nearly invisible in her ear.

She let out a huff. "Seriously?"

Uh oh. Had someone seen what had happened on the lot and she already knew all about it?

Shit. He had wanted to be the one to tell her. To at least try to explain. Then he could beg forgiveness or grovel or do whatever else it took to smooth things over with her.

And not just with her. With the studio too.

What if they couldn't shoot with Jamey's face like it was?

If he'd thrown off the production schedule . . . If he'd cost the movie thousands—hell, possibly hundreds of thousands of dollars—all because he'd been a jealous fool, an apology wasn't going to cut it.

What if they fired Sierra because of him?

Fuck. This was way worse than he'd ever imagined, and what he'd imagined was pretty bad.

The woman he loved might never forgive him for this. And she'd be justified in doing so.

As Sierra stood and started pacing the room while she listened to whatever the person on the other end of the line was saying, Rick sat.

He leaned forward in the chair, forearms braced on his knees, head down as he waited for his turn to speak with her.

"This is the worst possible time for this. You know that, right?" she asked.

That brought Rick's head up. He breathed in relief when he realized the bitter question wasn't directed at him, but at the person on the phone with her.

Of course, that didn't mean she wasn't talking about him, or at least about the situation he'd caused.

"Fine. I'll read it tonight and text you my decision when I'm done. Is that soon enough?"

Sierra listened for a moment.

"I know. Look for my text." She lowered the cell from her ear and finally glanced up at him.

"Everything all right?" he asked, dreading the answer.

"Yeah." She drew in a breath and let it out in a burst. "But I'm going to have to grab my food and lock myself in the bedroom to read a script. I'm sorry."

He remembered his whole reason for going to the lot tonight in the first place and stood. He drew the rolled pages he'd gone to retrieve out of the pocket in the leg of his cargo pants.

"This?" He handed the colored pages to her.

She let out a snort as she pulled take-out containers from the bag on the table. "No, but I need to do that too before tomorrow morning."

Locating her sushi roll and seaweed salad, Sierra also grabbed a set of chopsticks and a napkin and straightened.

Items in hand, she said, "I need to make a decision tonight about whether I want a role in a movie that won't start filming until next year. My agent sent the script to me the day before we flew out here to start production. I've just been too busy with this movie to read the script for the next one."

"Oh. Well, I guess it's a good thing. You're in demand, right?"

She frowned. "It's one more thing I don't need on my plate tonight, is what it is."

Sierra turned toward the bedroom and Rick took a step after her. "I really needed to talk to you about something."

She glanced back. "Can it wait? I haven't even opened this script yet and she's waiting for my text."

Feeling guilty for his relief over his reprieve, Rick nodded. "Yeah, sure. It'll wait."

"Thanks, babe." The smile she shot him would normally warm him straight through to his core.

Tonight, all it did was make his heart clench at the thought of losing this woman. "I love you," he said as she strode through the bedroom door.

"Love you back," she said as she closed the door between them.

The click of the door latch had Rick cussing beneath his breath.

He had to fix this. Somehow. And fast.

CHAPTER FIVE

The sun was up and glaring by the time Sierra walked out of the make-up trailer the next morning, making her squint behind her sunglasses.

She'd been up way too late the night before reading that damn script. The problem was, it was such a weird and convoluted plot she'd had to actually read the whole thing rather than just skim the beginning to get a gist of the story.

It was some sort of psychological thriller and dammit, that's what made it so tempting. She really needed to break out of the box she'd been pigeon holed in lately.

After a string of romance films, she should take this role because it was so different. But in this town different wasn't always better.

People made cookie cutter movies, each one looking like the last, because it was a sure thing. A formula guaranteed to return a profit.

If only her manager hadn't left the business a couple of months ago. She needed Roger's advice now.

She probably would have called him last night and asked his opinion anyway, even though he didn't work for her any longer, *if* it hadn't been the middle of the night on the east coast.

For now, she was on her own in making this career-changing decision.

How would her fans react if she took something so totally different from her norm?

She guessed she was going to find out. Late last night, when she'd finally gotten to the end—and holy hell what an ending it had been—she'd texted her agent that she was interested.

So there it was. In the middle of the night, tired and hungry because the sushi hadn't filled her up even a little bit—she'd made either the best or the worst decision of her career.

And she hadn't gotten around to studying the pages for today, so guess what she did in the makeup chair this morning...

It was going to be a hell of a day.

Inside her trailer, she frowned when one glance around the small space told her Rick wasn't inside.

In fact, she'd barely seen him recently.

He'd fallen asleep on the sofa in front of the television last night while she'd been in the bedroom reading. And though she felt horrible leaving him there, he looked as if he was sleeping so soundly she hadn't had the heart to wake him so he could move to the bed after she'd finished the script.

Then, this morning, she'd had her nose buried in the pages while he drove them to the lot. After a quick kiss, he'd sent her into the makeup trailer where she continued to study the pages.

They'd had time to speak barely a handful of words since the moment he'd come home with the take-out order last night.

How did other actresses do it? Make a relationship work with someone not in the business? If Rick's job weren't to be with her during every waking moment, she'd hardly ever see him.

She grabbed her cell phone, about to punch in a text to tell him she was out of makeup, when a knock had her stopping.

That was probably him. He always knocked. He'd said he didn't want to fling open the trailer door in case she was inside changing.

Polite to the core . . . or maybe Rick, who had an obvious jealous streak, just didn't want anyone walking by to see her half dressed.

She'd spent all day yesterday naked on the set, and millions were going to see her like that in the movie, but she appreciated the sentiment.

Smiling, she yanked open the door, but the silly joke she was going to deliver about her not letting strange men into her trailer died on her lips when she saw it wasn't him.

"They need you in a meeting," the young male PA said.

"A meeting?" She frowned. "I don't remember hearing about a meeting."

Had she missed a text or an email? She looked down at the cell phone that was still in her hand as the kid, who—God help her—looked young enough she could have birthed him, shook his head.

"It wasn't scheduled. The director just called it."

"Oh. Okay." Following the kid out, she pulled the door closed behind her.

Now she was really going to have to text Rick. She didn't want him getting to the trailer and not finding her there, or in makeup, or on the set.

He'd freak the hell out. Probably call for a lock down of the lot. Before she knew it there'd be air support and a team of his former SEAL friends scouring the place.

She'd been the recipient of their collective attention before and it was intense. Best to head off any problems right now.

She was trying to text and walk—a no-no, she knew—when the kid opened the door she hadn't realized they'd reached. He stepped to the side and she went through, hitting send on a text that was much shorter than she'd intended.

Meeting. Catch up after.

At least it would keep him from calling in the bloodhounds.

Did SEALs use bloodhounds? Doubtful. Hounds were more small town sheriff and prison guard type dogs.

Rick would probably use German Shepherds. At least that looked like the breed they used on that television show SEAL Team.

Sad how she got most of her real world knowledge from Hollywood. Sadder that so much of it was probably inaccurate.

But of course, Hollywood had it's own kind of reality.

She gave up on waiting for Rick's reply and lowered the cell. She raised her gaze and noticed the grave expression on the director's face.

But that wasn't what had her gasping. That came after she saw the mess that was Jamey's face.

"Oh my God. Are you all right?" All else forgotten—Rick's absence, Howard's expression—she rushed forward toward the man who looked nothing like he had yesterday when she'd left him.

Jamey waved away the concern. "I'm fine. It's nothing."

"Nothing?" Her eyes widened in shock as she got close enough to truly appreciate the colorful bruise. "Were you in a car accident?"

"Uh, no." He dropped his gaze away from hers.

What the hell was going on?

Confused, Sierra lowered herself into the seat next to him. She reached out and took both of his hands in hers.

They might have only met a short time ago, but she'd spent up to eighteen hours a day with this guy. They'd rolled around naked—or at least nearly naked. Why was he being so evasive with her now instead of answering a simple question?

"Tell me," she said.

Jamey glanced at the director.

Sierra followed his gaze. Howard was sitting there silent but obviously stewing. Did he not know either?

She turned back to Jamey and squeezed his hands.

"It was just a misunderstanding," he said.

A misunderstanding?

"You mean like a fight? Someone punched you?" she guessed.

"Yeah. Kinda," he said.

Turning his hands over in hers, she inspected his knuckles. They were perfect.

She lifted her gaze to look at his swollen face. "But you didn't punch back, did you?"

"No." He pulled his hands away from hers. "I told you. It was just a misunderstanding."

"A misunderstanding that is going to cost us weeks," Howard said.

Jamey shook his head. "No, it won't. It won't even cost us a day."

"Oh, really. And how do you figure that?" Howard asked.

"Makeup can cover the bruise," Jamey said.

Sierra nodded. "The bruise, but not that swelling. It's going to show."

"They can shoot me from the other side," Jamey

suggested.

"Oh, yeah. Great solution. We'll just always have you in profile for the next week or two." Howard rolled his eyes.

"Then we'll juggle the schedule. We shoot the flashback scenes now instead of next month. My character is at war. It won't look odd if I look a little beat up. Besides, under grease paint and in a helmet with night vision goggles on, no one will see."

Howard shook his head. "There are so many things wrong with that plan I can't even begin to tell you."

"Come on, Howard. Work with me here. Why can't we swap out the scenes?" Jamey asked.

"For one, we had planned on two dozen extras coming in for the big ambush scene next month, not tomorrow. That's besides the fact that it requires the entire crew travel to another state. That requires hotel rooms and the location itself, all of which are reserved for, as I've said, next month."

Sierra heard the sound of the door open and close behind her. She turned and saw Rick.

He must have seen her text and tracked down where the meeting was being held.

Not a surprise. He was like a bulldog with a bone, a real problem solver when it came to finding her. It was as endearing as it could be annoying sometimes. But right now, she had bigger things to worry about than why Rick was here in her meeting, or why he looked so grim about it.

She turned back to face Jamey. His gaze was also on Rick, until he dragged it away and focused on Howard. "I'll personally cover whatever the delay is going to cost."

Sierra heard Rick's sharp intake of breath but didn't turn. She was too busy waiting to see if Howard was going to take Jamey up on the offer. A delay in production could cost hundreds of thousands of dollars, depending on how long it lasted.

Howard let out a snort. "I think I'll take you up on that offer. Perhaps it will teach you to be a little more careful. For Christ's sake, Jamey, what were you thinking? Did you go out and get drunk and get in some bar brawl? Or hit on some girl with a jealous boyfriend?"

Jamey remained silent, accepting the dressing down but not responding to Howard's questions.

"I'm asking you what happened. I'd like an answer," Howard said, his tone sharp.

Jamey pressed his lips more tightly together, his body language broadcasting that he wasn't about to tell. "It doesn't matter. Just take the money and let's figure out what to do about saving as much time as we can."

"Oh, we'll do that. After you tell me," Howard said.

Rick stepped forward.

Sierra cringed. Of all times for him to not be his usual invisible but ever present self . . . This was definitely not the time for Rick to make himself the object of Howard's attention. Not when the man was livid.

Howard lifted a brow as his gaze landed on Rick. "Can I help you?"

"It's my fault. Not his," Rick said.

"What do you mean?" Sierra asked before Howard had a chance to.

"Rick—" Jamey's words were cut off as Rick held up one hand.

"No. I won't let you take the blame or bear the cost of my mistake." Rick turned from Jamey to Howard. "I punched him."

"Why?" Sierra asked.

Howard's eyes widened. "Yes, I'd like to know that too."

Rick drew in a breath that somehow seemed to make him look taller. Or maybe it was just that he'd straightened his spine, lifted his chin and held his head high. He was braced to face whatever came next, though Sierra didn't know why.

What the hell had happened? And when? He'd only gone out to get sushi. But he'd also stopped by the lot to get her pages . . .

Her gaze dropped to his right hand and she noticed the swell of bruising. He wasn't lying. He'd punched Jamey.

"I thought he was sleeping with Sierra." Rick added, "In real life. Not just the movie."

"What? Why would you think that?" She stood to face him. He might be taller, but she was madder.

"It's my fault." Jamey stood too. "I said

something that he misinterpreted."

Shocked, she spun to Jamey. "You told him we were sleeping together?"

"No. Of course not. Why would I do that when it's not true? I was on the phone and he overheard me talking about something else and thought I was talking about you." Jamey shook his head. "It doesn't matter. It's nobody's fault. It was just a mistake."

"I want you off my lot. Now." Howard's words had Sierra's head whipping around to see who he was talking to, though she really didn't need to see Howard's deadly glare leveled on Rick to know.

Rick nodded, eerily calm. "I understand. And I'll go. But not before Sierra's new security team arrives and I get them up to speed. They're on their way. It won't be more than an hour. I promise."

The whole time Rick focused on Howard, as if she wasn't even there though this most definitely involved her.

"What new security team?" she asked. "Who? And how did you know to bring them in?"

Finally, he glanced at her. "I wasn't going to let him take the blame for something I did, so this morning I got in touch with the team and told them I need some experienced operators here to replace me."

"SEALs?" Jamey asked, taking a step forward.

Rick smiled sadly. "Yeah. You're going to get your SEALs."

"Who's coming?" Sierra asked.

"Jon and Zane."

She frowned. "Shouldn't they be in Virginia Beach?"

"I was lucky. They happened to be at Coronado. They're coming today to get the lay of the land then they'll assign someone from their west coast operators to take over your security for the rest of the shoot."

"Holy shit." Jamey spun to Howard. "Do you realize what this means?"

"That I'm wasting a whole lot of valuable time listening to bullshit that is not getting my movie made?" Howard scowled.

"No. You're wrong about that. Do you even know who this guy is?"

"I figure he's Sierra's boyfriend as well as her security. Though I'm not really sure which came first, not that it matters."

Jamey shook his head. "He's a Navy SEAL. And so are his buddies who are coming today."

"And?" Howard asked.

"So is my character. Don't you see? They can help us." Jamey was visibly excited.

Howard cocked up one brow. "We have a military consultant."

Jamey shook his head. "Not a SEAL."

Howard shrugged. "What's the difference? Military is military."

Rick let out a snort as Sierra prayed he'd keep his mouth shut.

Getting tossed off this one movie was bad enough, but Howard could easily do worse than that. He was a powerful man with lots of friends. He could easily get Rick blackballed. Banned from any future movie sets.

Then where would they be?

She'd never see him. Hell, his behavior could affect her career too.

Producers and directors took many things into consideration when hiring an actress—her having a boyfriend and head of security with an obvious temper who destroyed the leading man's face in the middle of production would certainly be one of them.

Just thinking about Rick's behavior, what he'd done, how he could possibly think she would cheat on him, had her blood pressure rising.

She shot him a glare, as much to silence him from pissing off Howard any further, as to let him know how unhappy she was with him.

He pressed his lips together and thank God remained quiet.

"It's not the same," Jamey said. He spun to Rick. "Tell him. How many things do you see in movies and on television that are inaccurate?"

"It'd be easier to list the few things they get right."

"See!" Jamey threw his hands in the air. "We need him. And his friends. I'll pay them out of my own pocket if I have to."

Howard sent Jamey a glare. "You sure are eager

to spend your money. Apparently we paid you too much for this movie."

"I want it right." Jamey shook his head. "I don't care what it costs or if I don't make a penny, as long as it's accurate."

Howard let out a snort. "I'll remember your feelings next contract negotiation with your agent."

"If it'll help, I'll go over the script. No charge," Rick said. "And I can watch the dailies, check the equipment and the uniforms, even the battle strategies if you want and make a list of what I see wrong. I owe you at least that for all of this."

Howard focused on Rick. "I haven't decided yet if I'm going to even let you stay on the set, but if I do you'd be here on a probationary basis. You'd listen to me. Follow orders, no questions asked. And you're right, you would be doing this consulting for no charge to make up for what you're costing us in time and money because of your jealous fit."

"And you won't charge Jamey for the delay if I do this?" Rick asked. "I don't want him paying for my mistake."

"No, I won't take his money, even though he's all too eager to offer it up." Howard shot Jamey a glance.

Looking visibly relieved, Rick tipped his head in a nod. "Then I'll do it."

"What about your friends? Will they help too, you think?" Jamey asked, looking like a kid about to meet his favorite major league baseball player. "I'll pay them."

"I don't know. I can't answer for them, but we can ask." Rick shrugged. "You gotta understand that they're real busy. Zane mentioned having to be in Djibouti next week."

"Djibouti." Jamey spun back to Howard. "See? These guys are no shit, real deal military."

"Are you?" Howard asked Rick with a smirk, not looking as impressed as Jamey. "Are you really no shit, real deal military?"

Rick shot Jamey a glance, looking as if he was amused by the hero worship even as he enjoyed it just a little. "Yes, sir. I guess I am."

"Tell me, how many punches did it take you to do that to his face?" Howard tipped his head toward Jamey.

Rick's brows shot up at the question. "Um. One."

Howard pressed his lips together. "As much as I hate to say it, I wouldn't mind having a real SEAL on the set. And the fact you owe me doesn't hurt. But I want this understood. There will be no diva attitude. No taking time off. No complaining over long hours or too much time on your feet. You'll have to be present for all the military shoots and trust me, there will be long hours with no breaks and late nights."

Sierra could see Rick trying and failing to hide his amusement. "I'll be fine."

Howard drew in a breath and let it out loudly. "Okay. But you step out of line just once—"

"And I'm off the set," Rick finished Howard's

sentence. "I understand."

Scowling at being cut off, Howard shot Rick a glare before moving on to Jamey. "And you. You go to makeup and see what they can do with that face."

"Yes, sir." His lips twitching with a victorious smile, Jamey jumped to extend his hand to Rick. "Thanks for agreeing."

"Don't thank him," Howard raged. "You should fucking thank me. And all of you get out of my office. I've got to figure out how to salvage this schedule and convince the production department I haven't lost my mind."

"Thank you, Howard." Jamey shot him a crooked painful-looking smile as he moved toward the door Rick had opened. "This movie is going to take home an Oscar because of this. You'll see."

"It better," Howard shouted at their retreating backs.

Sierra hung behind. "I wanted to say I'm sorry. I had no idea any of that went down last night."

He lifted a brow. "I figured you didn't know by the look on your face when he walked in and told us. You're not that good of an actress."

Sierra frowned at the insult.

Howard continued, "But if I were you, I'd seriously consider the fact that he didn't bother to tell you that he might have destroyed your movie because he thought you were sleeping with your co-star."

An insult and now relationship advice? That

was rich coming from a man on his fourth marriage.

Even if his point was valid, it wasn't welcome, so Sierra didn't acknowledge it. "Text me when we're ready to shoot."

Without waiting for a reply she stepped outside into the light and slammed the door behind her. She was done with Howard and his comments.

Time to confront Rick. They had a lot to talk about.

CHAPTER SIX

"You didn't have to do that. Take the fall." In the bright light of outdoors, the bruising on Jamey's face was more prominent. More visible.

Rick hoped that make-up girl was good at her job because over the next few days, that bruise was only going to get even more colorful.

He shook his head. "Yeah, I did. It was my fault. He needed to know that."

"But I could have smoothed it over—" Jamey began.

"Listen, kid. You're playing a SEAL so you should know this. At the core of being a good Navy SEAL is knowing the right action and taking the right action. A good SEAL seeks and accepts responsibility for his own actions every fucking time, no matter what."

Jamey tipped his head. "So that's why you confessed."

Rick nodded. "That's why."

The kid looked bowled over. As if Rick had just delivered the secret to the universe.

Finally, he recovered enough to say, "At least Howard looked like he took it pretty well. I mean yeah, at first he threw you off the set, but now he's letting you stay around and consult."

Jamey's exuberance over Rick's being allowed to stay on the lot was palpable. He wished he could be as enthusiastic over his probationary status.

"I'm allowed to stay for now," Rick said.

He had experience both in and out of the military with people who asked for his opinion but didn't really want to hear what he had to say.

Rick could tell the director what was wrong with his movie, but he wasn't sure he'd like it, or do anything to correct it.

He was glad of one thing though—being allowed to stay on set meant he also got to remain near Sierra. That was good for many reasons . . .

Although maybe not so good right now. She'd come out of the door and was walking toward them. He could see she was fuming as she strutted toward him.

"What the hell, Rick?" She hadn't even reached them yet and she was already yelling at him.

"Uh, oh. She's mad." Jamey glanced sideways at Rick.

"Yup." Drawing in a deep breath he braced himself for the rampage.

He had it coming. He'd fucked up in a major way and now he had to face the consequences.

Good thing they had a suite. He had a feeling he might be sleeping on the sofa again tonight and this time not by choice.

"You thought I was cheating on you? With Jamey?"

"But it's really not his fault. You see he overheard me on the phone—" Sierra's deadly glare silenced Jamey's explanation in defense of Rick.

Rick shot him a glance. "Thanks, bud, but I'll handle this."

Jamey nodded and hooked a thumb in the direction of the make-up trailer. "Yeah, um, okay. I'm just gonna go see about covering this up."

"Good idea." Rick nodded.

Poor kid. He wasn't used to Sierra's rage. Rick, on the other hand, kind of liked it.

She was a passionate woman, in anger as well as in bed. Some fucked up Pavlovian kind of thing inside him saw a connection between the two.

As her chest rose and fell as she huffed with barely contained fury, Rick envisioned backing her up against the nearest wall and fucking her breathless.

He and Sierra had been together for a while and this wasn't their first fight. He knew her.

She was going to have to get out her rant. Only after she was done would she even hear what he had to say, so he widened his stance, folded his arms and settled in to wait until she was ready to listen to his apology.

Now that they were face to face, she laid into him.

She kept her voice down but there was no doubt people knew she was unhappy. That was obvious by the wide berth anyone passing by gave them, along with some interested glances before they pretended to look elsewhere.

Unhappy. Talk about an understatement.

She was fucking pissed is what she was and Rick did his best to control his burgeoning hard-on as she went on and on.

"Are you even listening to me?" she asked, taking a step closer.

Busted. He had been but she'd circled back to the same points three times about how irresponsible he was and how this could harm her career and how could he ever think she'd cheat on him—he'd heard it all the first time so he'd kind of zoned out.

"I'm listening."

"Then why don't you look like it?" she accused.

Because she was the academy award winning actor and he wasn't?

Rick kept that thought to himself. "Because there is nothing you can say that I haven't already thought and agonized over. I've beat myself up since last night and it didn't help or change a thing. The best thing I can do is help get this production back on track and try to minimize the damage I caused."

She crossed her arms over her chest, a doubt-filled expression shading her oh-so-expressive features. "And how are you going to do that?"

"Actually, I have a couple of ideas." He honestly did. It had been one of the things he'd been thinking about—besides stripping her naked and pounding into her—while he hadn't been listening to Sierra.

She quirked up one pretty eyebrow. "Well, you'd better hope whatever you've cooked up works or this movie, and possibly my career too, are fucked."

God, he loved when she cussed. He somehow controlled the smile that threatened to emerge when she dropped the F-bomb and said, "I'll make it work."

He'd been well trained. Taught that if plan A doesn't work, than you'd better have a plan B, and then a C, because failure was not an option. He was a damn Tier One operator, for God's sake.

After all that he'd encountered in his decade in the SEALs, if he couldn't solve this problem then he should turn in his trident.

Sierra should realize that. She'd known him for long enough. Had seen first hand how he didn't give up easily on something that was important to him. And this was. *She* was.

Judging by her expression, he was going to have to prove that.

He was about to elaborate on his plan—

preliminary though it was—when his cell vibrated in his pocket.

"Shit. Hang on. It could be the guys." In spite of her scowl at the interruption, Rick pulled the cell out of his pocket and glanced at the display. It was Jon calling.

"Hello."

"Hey, man. We're at the gate and they won't let us in."

"Yeah. I know. I didn't have time to put you on the list. Hang on. I'll be right there to get you."

"All right. We'll be here."

Rick lowered the phone as the call disconnected. "Jon and Zane are here."

"Howard's letting you stay on as my security—unless you fuck up again. We don't need your friends." Sierra scowled.

"Actually, we might."

"Why?" she asked.

"All part of my plan." He smiled. She did not.

"What plan?"

"The plan to fix this." And he wouldn't rest until he did just that.

She blew out a breath. "All right. Go do what you want. You will anyway."

Her final words, muttered as she turned away from him, had Rick reaching out and grabbing her arm. "Hey."

"What?" She finally raised her gaze to meet his.

So many words were on the tip of his tongue.

That he loved her. That they were going to be okay. That he'd fix this.

The words stayed right where they were—unspoken. Instead he reached out and pulled her close with one hand on the back of her neck.

He pressed a hard deep kiss to her mouth. A kiss he took deeper when he angled his head and thrust his tongue between her lips.

She kissed him back, in spite of the shocked expression he saw on her face when he pulled back.

"I thought we were keeping us quiet," she said, glancing around them to see who'd seen.

He let out a laugh. "Yeah, well, I think the jig is up on that. I'm going to go get them at the gate."

Looking a whole lot softer, less hard, less angry than she had before that kiss, Sierra nodded. "Okay."

Rick would have to remember that. Next fight, instead of talking, he'd just kiss her. It sounded like a good plan to him.

Now on to his other plan. The one that he hoped would save this movie. And his ass.

CHAPTER SEVEN

Rick couldn't help but smile when he saw the achingly familiar figures of his friends waiting for him at the gate.

He'd been away from home, from them, for too long. Seeing them again, here, reminded him of that. He was and always had been an east coast guy . . . or he had been until Sierra entered his life.

His friends were in their typical poses. Jon was leaning against the bumper of the SUV, arms crossed as he visually surveyed his surroundings through the mirrored lenses of his sunglasses. The difference was instead of searching the horizon for the enemy, now the only thing he'd find is the rolling hills of Hollywood in the distance.

Conversely, Zane's head was down as he

scrolled through his cell phone, though Rick supposed now that Zane was married he wasn't reading texts from his harem of girls like he would have been years ago.

Rick passed the guard at the gate with a quick nod and moved directly to his teammates.

Smiling, he strode forward. "Damn, I've missed your ugly faces."

"No more than we've missed yours." Jon slapped Rick on the back.

Zane put his phone down long enough to extend a hand to Rick. "Dude. Good seeing you again."

"You too. How's married life?" Rick asked Zane.

"Good. You should try it."

Pfft. If he and Sierra made it through the current cluster fuck he might think about it. Rick kept that to himself and deflected the conversation. "So how's things at home?"

"Your sister is spoiling the hell out of my kid." Jon smiled.

"No surprise there." Rick laughed. Darci loved kids. "The only surprise is that she isn't having one of her own yet."

Jon smiled. "Not for lack of trying, knowing Chris."

Zane, back on his phone, let out a snort of a laugh at Jon's joke. Rick however didn't find it amusing.

Appalled, Rick shook his head. "Dude. No. That's my sister and my friend you're talking about.

TMI."

Jon rolled his eyes. "Whatever. They're married now so get used to it. Anyway . . ." Jon tipped his head toward the lot and the gate they had yet to pass through. "What's happening here? What's going on that you need our guys for security?"

So much had happened in the past twelve hours, Rick didn't know how to explain it all. But he knew he did have to start with an apology.

"Yeah, about that. I'm sorry you came all the way here from San Diego to meet with me, but it looks like I won't need your help. At least not with that particular situation."

"No worries. We were heading this way anyway. We have a meeting at Port Hueneme early tomorrow, then we figured we could grab a red-eye out of LAX."

"Hueneme," Rick repeated, intrigued why the guys would be there having meetings. "That sounds interesting."

"It is. Very. And if you weren't all tied up here you might have been a part of it." The smirk on Zane's face told Rick he was being teased.

Jon laughed. "You're trying to make him envious of us? Look around you. He gets to spend all day surrounded by this." Jon swung an arm to indicate what was just beyond the gate.

It was surreal. Hollywood had a version of reality all its own. The movie lot was a microcosm of that. Things looked real enough if you didn't look too hard past the surface to find it was all fake.

But just the mechanics of it was fascinating to an outsider. At least it had been too Rick his first few times on the lot as Sierra's full time security. After they'd found her stalker and he didn't have to be on alert and on watch for snipers, that is.

Golf carts zipping between pedestrians, some transporting Hollywood A-listers. Gorgeous women. The occasional horse or camel. Costumes and vehicles from every era . . .

How so many people, working on so many different projects and spending such ungodly amounts of money could all occupy and function within the fenced confines of the same space was mind-boggling.

That aspect reminded Rick a bit of a military base in a warped, alternate reality kind of way.

Yet none of it made him stop missing his friends or the old days in the teams . . . Which brought him to his idea.

"There is something I want to talk to you about though. Something you might have some insight on."

"Sure." Jon tipped his dark head. "Shoot."

Zane lifted his chin and glanced toward the gate and guardhouse. "We gonna do this standing here or head out for a drink somewhere? Looks like this place is harder to get into than the base."

Rick laughed. "It can be. But don't worry. For now, I still have the power to get you onto the lot *and* we can have a drink."

Sierra didn't have booze in her trailer, at least

nothing he and the guys would drink since he didn't count pink wine as booze, but he knew Jamey did.

He also knew the kid would gladly serve it up if it meant meeting some more real life SEALs. But more than that, he needed a copy of the script. More than one if he could get his hands on them—one for each of them.

Their collective brainpower might be the only way to figure out this mess.

It had worked before in far more critical situations. Times when it was their lives on the line rather than just a couple of hundred thousand dollars.

Christ. He couldn't even think about that large of a sum without having heart palpitations.

Turning to Jon and Zane he said, "Come on. We can drive through with my ID."

Time to get this show on the road—literally.

CHAPTER EIGHT

Sierra had watched Jeannie perform magic in the past.

She was like Rembrandt but she worked in makeup rather than paint.

Her canvases had included some of this generations most famous actors . . . but even Jeannie was no match for the destruction Rick had wrought on Jamey's face with one punch.

On some level Sierra knew that the fact Rick could do such damage with his bare hands should scare the shit out of her.

It didn't. She knew he'd never lay a hand on her.

Apparently her co-star was another story.

She drew in a breath and let it out in a loud

angry huff.

Airbrush in hand, Jeannie cut her dark brown gaze sideways. "I'm not done yet."

"It's not going to help." Sierra scowled.

Professional makeup might cover the discoloration, but that swelling . . . Nope. No way.

Jeannie let out a *humph*. "Oh, ye of little faith."

It wasn't just faith in Jeannie that Sierra was lacking at the moment.

It was faith in Rick. Their relationship. Their future.

She loved him. But if he didn't trust her after all these years, what future could they have? She wasn't going to live in fear of the next time he went into a jealous rage.

The next guy might not be so understanding. Then there'd be lawsuits and media scandal . . .

"Stop." Jamey's single word command brought her head up.

Sierra noticed his gaze on her in the mirror. "Stop what?"

"Stop blaming Rick. It wasn't his fault."

"I beg to differ. So would Jeannie I'm sure, since Rick has made her job a thousand times harder for the next couple of weeks."

"Don't bring me into this. I love a good challenge. It's been too long since I had to do anything besides make beautiful people look more beautiful. Give me a good zombie movie and I'm a happy girl."

Sierra rolled her eyes. Jeannie might have a soft spot for Rick, but right now, Sierra didn't share it.

Jamey turned in the chair to face her. "I want to tell you exactly what happened."

"Fine. I'll listen. But turn back around and let Jeannie finish her job."

He nodded and let Jeannie spin the chair. "So I was on the cell phone. I don't remember the exact words I used but all Rick heard me say was something like *she's a sweet ride* and that I was going to take her for another spin and make her mine. I didn't care who she belonged to."

That did sound pretty bad and confusing.

Sierra frowned. "Who were you talking about?"

"A vintage motorcycle I'm trying to buy."

She rolled her eyes. Men were weird. All of them. "That still doesn't justify what Rick did. You never said my name, right?"

"No, but—"

"There's no *but*. He jumped to conclusions. Irrational, ridiculous conclusions." That part was bad enough, but then he went and punched Jamey rather than talking it out with her or him. It was all too much. "He's possibly set this movie back by weeks."

"Maybe not." Rick's deep voice behind her had Sierra spinning toward the door.

She had to admit, he did look contrite standing there in the doorway and looking too big for the small space.

Gone was his usual confident cockiness. In its

place was an expression of remorse mingled with determination.

He spared her a brief glance before his gaze moved to Jamey. "Hey, would it be okay if we hung in your trailer for a couple of hours?"

"We who?" Jamey spun around again and leaned forward, making Jeannie have to step backward out of his way for the second time.

"Me and my buddies."

Jamey's eyes widened. "The SEALs? They're here?"

"Yes, the SEALs. You mind? We need someplace private to talk and brainstorm. And we need a copy of the script if you've got one we can borrow."

"Sure. Definitely. Mine's in the binder in my trailer. Make yourself at home."

"Cool. Thanks." Rick tipped his head toward Jamey before directing his focus toward Sierra. "Can we borrow your script too?"

"Why?" She narrowed her eyes at him, trying to determine what he and his friends could be planning. "What are you up to?"

"I told you before. I caused this cluster fuck. Now, hopefully with Jon and Zane's help, I'm gonna fix it."

Could he fix it? And how?

Of all the skills and experience she knew he and his SEAL friends had, movie production was not one of them. At least, not that she knew of, anyway.

Maybe he figured if he and the guys did a real

good job correcting the military stuff, Howard would forgive him.

That wouldn't help fix Jamey's face any faster but it was better than doing nothing, she guessed. "Yes, you can borrow my script. It's in my trailer."

"Thank you. Any chance you can get us a third copy this morning?" he asked.

"Um, I'm not sure. Production is pretty strict about access to the script. The studio doesn't want anything leaking."

Sierra sighed when she saw Rick's brow shoot up. She didn't ask why, because she could easily guess what he was thinking.

"And yes, I realize you all had all sorts of top secret clearance in the military but that doesn't matter here."

"I hate to say it, but she's right, man," Jamie said. "It's a different world in here. Studios operate by their own set of rules."

"Oh, believe me. I know." Rick blew out a breath. "Okay, we'll deal with sharing the two copies."

"Just don't take them off the lot. We could get in trouble," Sierra said, starting to worry this was one more thing Rick might do wrong that would blow back on her.

Rick rolled his eyes. "I won't leave the lot. I promise. We'll be in Jamey's trailer for the next couple of hours."

As Rick reached for the doorknob, Jamey leaned forward again, about to stand. "Wait. Let me give you the key."

Rick shook his head. "No worries. Those locks are child's play."

"Oh, that's wonderful to hear," Sierra said with as much sarcasm as she could muster.

"Not yours, princess." He forced a humorless smile as he used the nickname he knew she hated. "I beefed up the lock on your trailer the day we arrived."

"Really?" *Humph.* What else did Rick do without her knowing while she was occupied elsewhere?

The possibilities were intriguing as well as frightening.

Jamey ignored both her comment and Rick's as he planted both hands on the arms of the chair, like he was about to stand. "Wait. I want to come with—"

"No." She and Jeannie said the single word simultaneously.

"I need a little more time to cover that." Jeannie indicated the swollen mess that was Jamey's formerly perfect profile.

"You definitely want your face to look as good as it can to keep Howard calm, since we're not sure if whatever plan these guys can come up with is going to work," Sierra added.

She caught Rick's scowl over her doubt out of the corner of her eye.

"Okay." As Jamey let out a sigh and eased back into the chair, Rick opened the door.

"And on that note," he said. "I think I'll be going."

"I'll see you in my trailer in a few minutes," Jamey called after him.

Without turning around, Rick waved one hand in the air before closing the door behind him.

"How much longer?" Jamey asked Jeannie, tapping his feet against the floor like a kid unhappy to be in the barber chair.

Sierra laughed. "I hope it's soon. He looks like he's going to bolt."

"I know." Jeannie sighed and stepped back, turning the chair and Jamey to face Sierra. "What do you think?"

Normally when asked a question like that, she'd barely look, say *fine* and move on.

Not today.

She stepped forward, bending at the knees to get a look at his face from different angles. Any angle the camera might capture if the director chose to try to shoot the scenes scheduled for today.

It was a new scene, so continuity from the prior day's shoot wouldn't normally be a huge issue. But today, a good portion of Jamey's face was larger than it used to be. The difference in his appearance was going to stand out like a sore thumb in comparison with what they shot when his face was normal.

"I don't know," Sierra said, pressing her lips into a tight line. "Maybe we can get away with it *if* they get creative with the camera angles.

"Which scene were you supposed to shoot this morning?" Jeannie asked.

The morning, which was already almost gone? Sierra ignored that fact and tried to remember all that was on today's call sheet. "The wedding scene was supposed to be this morning."

Which meant all those extras brought in to fill the chairs for the ceremony were sitting around getting paid to do nothing. Howard must be losing his mind.

Jeannie let out a short laugh. "Too bad the groom can't wear the veil, huh?"

"No kidding." She could only hope Howard thought the makeup covered enough.

"So can I go?" Jamey asked.

Sierra knew exactly where he wanted to go. To his trailer to be with Rick and the guys.

He wasn't going to get there if she had anything to say about it.

When had leading men gotten so young that she felt like their mother? She didn't want to know the answer to that. She suspected they seemed younger only because she continued to get older.

That was a concern for another day. A day when there weren't dozens of extras getting paid to sit around and wait.

"You can't go back to your trailer. There's an entire crew on the clock plus a bunch of extras, all costing money while we find out if we're going to be able to shoot today or not. You need to go to Howard's office and see what he thinks. If he says we can get away with the scheduled scene, I need to go to wardrobe and get into that wedding gown."

Her unhappy co-star pouted.

"Come on. I'll go with you to Howard's office. We'll convince him everything is fine, we'll get to set, late but not too bad, and get this damn movie back on track. Deal?"

"Yeah." Jamey moved toward the door literally dragging his feet.

Sierra shook her head at him. "Hey. How about I text Rick and ask when Jon and Zane will have to leave? Then we'll make sure you get to at least meet them before they go."

"Really?" He brightened. "You'd do that for me?"

She patted his good cheek. "Yes, Jamey. Anything to make you happy."

If she'd learned anything over the years, it was that happy heroes made for good footage. The way things were going, this film needed every advantage it could get.

"Cross your fingers this works and Howard let's us shoot," she said to Jeannie as she reached to close the door behind her.

Jeannie smiled. "Fingers and toes crossed. And I'll be there personally for touch-ups, just in case."

"Good. Thanks." Sometimes it took the women on the set to keep the men on track. And sometimes a bit of luck didn't hurt either.

CHAPTER NINE

Another snort came out of Zane as he whipped the pencil out from behind his ear and attacked the page in the script binder that had apparently offended him.

Rick had seen pretty early on that he couldn't give Jon or Zane free rein with a pen. They were going to have the pages so marked up they'd be illegible.

In an effort to minimize the damage, he'd scrambled and come up with a couple of pencils instead.

Thank God he remembered the guard at the gate always had a crossword puzzle in front of him. Luckily he also had a couple of pencils and was willing to part with them.

Hell, Rick would buy the guy a year's supply worth of brand new #2s. Anything if it meant he could win back the director's trust by correcting all the military stuff the original script had wrong.

But it would require more than correcting mistakes to get this movie back on track.

He'd been in that makeup trailer. He'd seen Jamey's face. The makeup wasn't going to be good enough. Jeannie and Sierra might have hope, but he feared it was wishful thinking on their part.

Movies went from the big screen where everything was blown up way larger than life, almost directly to streaming on high definition wall size televisions. There was no room for flaws in today's blockbuster films.

Critics, fans, somebody was going to notice that in one scene Jamey looked normal and in the next his face was blown up. The director would realize that. And that was why Rick needed a plan.

They were going to have to figure out a way to film the flashback stuff, which luckily were mostly military scenes. Right in Rick's wheelhouse.

He turned back to Jon, who was a lot more calmly tackling his half of the script than Zane was.

Rick had taken the pages out of Sierra's binder and divided them up between Jon and Zane, then he'd kept Jamey's for himself, so all three of them could work simultaneously with only two copies.

Unfortunately, he wasn't getting a whole lot of reading done. Concentration was near impossible.

His mind was all over the place. Thinking.

Planning. Worrying—mostly worrying. About the movie. About Sierra.

He pushed the worries aside and asked, "What do you guys think so far?"

The flashback scenes were scattered throughout the movie, so both Jon and Zane should have been able to read a portion of the military parts at least, even having only half the script each.

Zane raised his gaze. "I think whoever wrote this thing should be court marshaled."

Jon snorted. "Can't disagree there."

"I meant, what do you think about the location requirements?"

"Like for the ambush scene?" Jon asked.

"Yeah."

He shrugged. "It seems pretty generic to me. It could probably be shot anywhere. Where did you say he had it planned?"

"I don't know. All I know is the location isn't available until next month but we need to shoot this now. This week." Rick remembered the other half of the equation and ran a hand over his face in frustration. "Shit. He's also got extras lined up for that scene, but not until next month, so there's no guarantee they'll be available early either."

"Extras to play the SEAL team?" Zane asked with obvious derision.

"Yeah, I assume. But also to play the enemy, I suppose." What the fuck did Rick now? He was just guessing at this point. Maybe it would help to have Jamey here with them.

"Hmm. I wonder . . ." Jon's comment captured Rick's attention.

"Wonder what?" he asked.

"You thinking the same thing I'm thinking?" Zane smiled at Jon.

"I don't know. Maybe." Jon grinned.

"Well, would someone like to tell me?" Rick huffed out a breath.

"San Clemente Island," Zane said.

San Clemente. One of the Channel Islands located off the coast of California. The Navy had been using it for training for decades.

Rick's eyes widened. "Holy shit. That would be perfect. You think we could get approval?"

Zane stood and pulled his cell out of his pocket. "Let's see."

"Who are you calling?" Rick watched in amazement as Zane scrolled through his contact list. Who was on there? He'd love to see.

"The director of the National Park Service owes me a favor."

Rick drew back, suitably impressed. "Damn."

Jon laughed. "Yeah, it's handy having Zane living in D.C. and racking up favors. Now for those extras you talked about. I have an idea."

"I can't wait to hear it." If it was half as good as Zane's idea about the location, they might be able to pull this thing off.

"How many days we talking here?" Jon asked.

Rick glanced at the script. "I'd have to ask to be

sure, but I can estimate."

He'd been on enough sets with Sierra to have a feel for how long things took.

This would be his first movie with military operation scenes but he knew the general timeline. Knew about how long the rest of the movie would take to shoot. Knew the studio would be too cheap to spend too much time and budget on scenes that weren't going to be a major part of the movie.

This was first and foremost an emotional flick. Not a war movie.

"Maybe two days? Three max, I guess?" Rick lifted a shoulder.

Jon nodded, looking pleased with that answer. "You know we were just at Coronado."

"Yeah." Rick nodded, not sure where Jon was going with this.

"They've got a class that's graduating tomorrow. You know those guys are going to take liberty right after."

Rick's brow furrowed in a frown. "Wait. Are you suggesting using the graduates as extras for the movie? You think they'd really do it?"

"Think back to when we graduated. We were so hyped up and full of ourselves. Yeah, they'll go home thinking they want to spend time with their families, but after two days they'll have enough. I would have loved to hang out with the guys from my class instead of sitting home jonesing for action."

Rick had to agree. Going back to the normal

world—aside from being able to sleep for days if he wanted to—had been an anti-climatic conclusion to what had felt, then, like the most momentous accomplishment of his life.

Jon was right. He would have loved to hang out with people who understand what he'd gone through because they'd been through it too.

"Besides," Jon continued, "after graduation, they'll be looking for pussy and booze. Being able to say they were in a big blockbuster movie, and getting paid to do it . . . Hell, that's a surefire recipe for getting laid and they'll have some extra cash in their pocket to go out and have fun with."

As piece by piece fell into place, Rick's pulse sped. This could actually work.

"You might be right." He knew if he brought his teammates in they'd solve this problem.

"Of course, I am. And as soon as Zane gets off the phone with the parks guy, we'll have him call Coronado and see about ordering us a team of brand new SEALs." Jon stood and slapped Rick on the back. "Now, did you mention us getting a drink somewhere?"

Rick let out a laugh. "Yeah. You earned it. And if this all pans out, you definitely deserve more than a drink."

He stood and moved to the cabinet. He'd replace Jamey's bottle later but right now, they all deserved a drink for the work they'd accomplished so far.

It was a good plan, but a plan that depended on so many moving parts it could just as easily fizzle and die as soar.

Yup. Rick sure as hell needed a drink.

It was time to celebrate the small wins now . . . in case it all fell apart later.

CHAPTER TEN

"I can't believe he won't let us shoot. He sent all those extras home and canceled everything on the call sheet for today for what? I look fine." Jamey ranted as he and Sierra walked toward his trailer.

"No, Jamey. Howard is right. You don't look the way you did for yesterday's shots. It's going to show."

"So use CGI or something. They do all this fucking amazing stuff for Sci Fi movies. Why can't they do that for this?"

"Because CGI isn't in the budget for this movie." Neither was losing weeks of filming because of Jamey's broken cheekbone thanks to her Spec Op-trained boyfriend's jealous temper and quick fists.

The anger started to glow again inside her chest.

"We could have worked around it. Shot something else today so continuity isn't an issue. Howard's just being a fucking dick."

Production of major pictures like theirs couldn't pivot on a dime. Jamey should know that. He was just being irrational because he was pissed.

She was pretty pissed herself, but not enough to forget where they were. "Shh. Get inside before you start saying shit that could get you fired," she warned.

Jamey scowled. "He's not going to fire me. We've got too many hours shot already."

Stranger things had happened in this business and Sierra wasn't going to take a chance on sinking this film. She climbed the few steps and yanked open the door of Jamey's trailer.

He followed her up, but was blocked from entering as she was stopped dead in the doorway by the sight that greeted her.

It looked more like a war room than a set trailer. Not that she knew exactly what a war room looked like from personal experience but she'd watched enough military TV shows and movies to recognize this resembled one.

Zane was on the phone. Jon and Rick were clustered around the mirror. Upon closer inspection she saw Jon was drawing on the surface with a black marker.

Rick leaned in, a red marker in his hand and

added a few circles to whatever it was they were drawing.

"Wow. What's going on?" Jamey's excited exclamation had Rick turning toward the door.

Rick grinned and hooked a thumb toward Jon. "Jamey Garret, meet Jon Rudnick. And that guy on the cell currently convincing someone that he needs to get us approval to film your scene in Channel Islands National Park with actual SEALs as your extras is Zane Alexander."

Jamey moved Sierra over with a hand on each of her shoulders and moved toward the mirror as if in a daze. "Holy shit. And what's this?"

"The layout for the op." Jon took over the explanation from Rick.

"What op?"

"The one in your script. The scene where you get ambushed." Rick tipped a chin toward the papers scattered on the table.

What had been a neatly bound script in a binder was now a mess. And without even looking, Sierra had a bad feeling it was her script Rick had ripped apart and marked up.

She didn't have time to check as Jon started to explain in more detail to Jamey what he'd scribbled on the mirror.

It might have been hieroglyphics for all she knew, but Jon and Rick seemed to be able to interpret its meaning.

"See here?" Rick pointed. "This is the SEAL team. The good guys. They'll come in on Zodiacs at night under cover of darkness."

"*Not* in the broad daylight like you guys had it in the script," Jon added. "We checked. There's a new moon rising in a few days, which is perfect because we'd never go in during a full moon unless it was some kind of QRF situation and absolutely necessary."

"QRF?" Jamey asked.

"Quick reaction force," Rick answered.

"Anyway, the good guys hit the beach while the bad guys are set up for an ambush here." Jon marked the spot with an X.

"That's where the attack happens that puts your character in the hospital and gives him all the PTSD and injuries and shit," Rick jumped in. "I figure you can definitely film the hospital scenes with your face messed up. And, since you'll be wearing NVGs, a helmet and grease paint, you can shoot the ambush scene too."

"And that's where Zane's phone call comes in," Jon continued. "If he gets approval—and judging by that smile on his face he's going to get it—we might be able to get the new SEAL class from Coronado as your extras. He already got us approval to use San Clemente Island for the location."

"So no need to worry about the logistics of shooting the flashback scenes this week. We've got the location and hopefully the extras all covered." Rick grinned. "You can film this starting in a couple of days, bruised face and all."

What the hell? Sierra stood, amazed. How the hell had Rick managed all this?

Even though the testosterone in the small space was nearly overwhelming, Sierra took a step closer. "Wait. Hold on a minute. We're going to film on San Clemente Island? And with real SEALs as extras?"

"Not *we*. It won't be you, princess. This is for Jamey's flashbacks to battle. Page fifty-one." Rick tipped his head toward the remains of the script.

"Yes. I know what scene you're talking about, but it wasn't written like this at all."

"It was written wrong," Jon said flatly, leaving no room for argument.

"All right. It's a done deal." Zane, finally off his phone call, joined the group. "Hey, Sierra," he added as casually as if he hadn't just pulled off a miracle.

"Um, hi."

"What do you mean a done deal? We got permission?" Rick asked.

"Permission and about two dozen volunteers."

"Really?" Rick's eyes widened.

"I called the Master Chief. He asked the class and they are all in. He wants to be in the film too." Zane grinned.

Jon slapped Rick in the gut with the back of his hand. "Told you they'd want to do it."

"Wait? You're serious. We're going to be filming with actual SEALs?"

"They will be tomorrow as soon as they stand on the grinder and get that trident. Yup." Zane nodded.

They might as well have been talking in another language. Sierra didn't know what grinders and tridents had to do with anything, but she did know movies. She lifted one hand. "You're all forgetting one thing."

Three sets of eyes turned to her.

"Howard has to agree to all of this. Not just Howard, but the production department. There's a lot of planning and a lot of people involved in making a movie this size and they don't move quickly."

"Almost as many people and as much planning as a mission?" Zane dropped that little criticism against her protest with a smirk.

Sierra let out a breath. "Yes, I know. You guys used to do shit like this all the time."

Jon raised one finger. "Actually, we still do."

"Fine. But this is Hollywood and—"

"And it's a different world and we play by different rules here," Jamey interrupted her, finishing her thought. "I know that, but it's worth a try. Isn't it?"

The eager hope and excitement radiating from him had her nodding. "Yeah, it's worth a try."

His face broke out into a grin, before he winced and fingered his visibly swollen injury. He was hurting still but, as much as she hated to admit it, Rick was right. Jamey's injury wouldn't matter for the flashback scenes.

"All right, if we're going to go into Howard with this, we need a plan of how to present it. You guys might know all this stuff." She waved a hand at the mirror with a flourish. "But I know this business and I particularly know Howard, so this is how it's going to go . . ."

With any luck, they'd win this battle. They had to. Right now, it was their only hope of saving this movie and all their reputations. Possibly their careers.

CHAPTER ELEVEN

It was dark. Dark and eerily quiet.

That was the overwhelming sensation Sierra got as she stood on the island.

After being surrounded by the lights of Los Angeles, and before that Miami, to be somewhere this completely dark was disconcerting.

Those were bustling cities at night, lit by neon and streetlights, buildings and vehicles all filled with noisy active people.

This—this was what amounted to a deserted island. No electric lights. No buildings in sight. No people save for the movie crew and actors. But at least they wouldn't have to worry about locking down the street or the back of the shot like they usually did when filming in public locations.

She'd never paid all that much attention to the

moon before. Perhaps to admire a particularly big and bright one if she happened to see it, but not enough to miss it when it wasn't there. She sure as hell missed it tonight.

Even the presence of a few dozen SEALs couldn't make this place feel less deserted or creepy on the dark moonless night. It would make a great location for a horror movie.

Memories from too many hours during her youth spent watching that particular genre had Sierra moving a little closer to the monitor, the only source of light in her immediate vicinity.

The prop manager already stood there, watching the screen as Jamey did a sound check and a light check.

Normally a stand-in would be on hand to do that for the star. Tonight, they were running short on stand-ins but long on Navy SEALs, so Jamey stood in for the checks—and looked as thrilled as a kid on Christmas morning to be doing so.

This had to be the oddest shoot of her life.

"You think these guys are really going to be able to pull this off?" the prop guy asked, angling his head to glance at her.

God, she hoped so. This whole elaborate and unlikely scheme was her boyfriend's idea. It had better work.

She couldn't say that exactly, so instead she decided to be upbeat. "I think so. Why not?"

"Well for one thing, they're not actors."

Rick stepped up to them, invisible until he

emerged like a specter out of the darkness and into the glow of the monitor. "And they're not acting. They're doing exactly what they've been trained to do for the past two years. Fuck, after you work with these guys you'll never want to work with civilian extras again, because there is one thing these men do better than anyone else. That's follow orders and work as a team. Quick and precise."

"Places!"

"Speaking of following orders. Gotta go." Rick grinned beneath the multicolored grease paint covering his face.

The white of his teeth flashed from within his dark camouflaged face before he turned and disappeared completely into the darkness. The only evidence of his existence was the crunch of his boots on the sand until that too disappeared.

The prop manager shook his head. "This better turn out to be one fucking amazing scene. Like Academy Award for Best Cinematography kind of great. Do you know how much the props they insisted on cost us?"

There didn't seem to be a whole lot of props. They were on an island. Sierra shook her head. "No."

He let out a snort. "Let's just say four-tube night vision goggles don't come cheap. And having them was a deal breaker apparently. He refused to let us use the two-tube."

She frowned. "Rick did? Why?"

"The characters are written as being part of SEAL Team Six and apparently they only use the four-tube. I was told if I wanted to *fuck it up and look like an amateur* I should use two-tube NVGs instead of four. But if I wanted to do it right, I'd better get four-tubes. I believe that was the exact quote from your boyfriend."

She cringed at the word boyfriend. Although this discussion did help her understand why Rick continuously huffed and grumbled while they watched certain military TV shows and movies.

Sierra lifted a shoulder. "He lived this life for a decade so I guess he should know."

"I guess he should." The prop manager watched the monitor. "I have to admit, it does look fucking cool."

She watched the wide shot of the team speeding toward the shore in a boat. "Yeah, it does."

"And they did save us money on some things. The SEALs are wearing their own uniforms so I didn't have to get dozens of those in all the various sizes, which is always a pain in the ass. And somehow they managed to get us those Navy boats on loan. That would have been a bitch coming up with a couple of those on such short notice."

"Wow." She had to wonder how many favors Zane called in to get the use of actual Navy boats, on top of the two-dozen men in uniform.

"Hell, they're even carrying their own weapons. Loaded with our blanks since I didn't trust them."

"Didn't trust them how?" she asked.

"I don't know if they were pulling my leg or not, but your boyfriend and his two friends seemed too damned excited while they were talking about how cool it would be to shoot the scene using live ammo." The prop manager let out a snort. "Crazy mother fuckers."

She was seeing a whole other side of Rick's life. One she hadn't fully grasped or appreciated until tonight.

It was definitely an eye opener.

She tracked the action on the monitor. Fifteen SEALs plus Jamey jumped out of the two rubber boats and ran onto the shore. Somewhere, the other extras were hidden, playing the bad guys about to ambush Jamey's unit.

Sierra was appreciating how real it all looked just as an explosion rocked the ground beneath her feet. It threw her off balance and sent her landing on her ass in the sand.

With a curse, the prop manager reached down to help her up. "You okay?"

"Yeah. I think so," she said as she tried to brush damp sand off her clothes.

"I knew I shouldn't have agreed to let the SEALs rig the explosion."

Her eyes widened. Maybe she should have stayed in the hotel.

CHAPTER TWELVE

Next to Rick, Sierra yawned wide as she slumped low in the seat and cradled her extra large coffee in both hands.

"You could have stayed in bed, you know."

They'd filmed last night until zero-dark thirty, breaking just a couple of hours before sunrise.

She blew out a *pfft*. "Are you crazy? I'm not missing these dailies. Howard's going to decide if this whole scheme of yours is a success or a failure based on this footage."

Rick had been thrilled when he'd been told he'd be allowed to sit in and watch the dailies from last night's shoot.

What he wasn't as thrilled about was what Sierra had just said about Howard and his decision.

This was raw, unedited footage. How good

could it be? Even he knew how important editing was.

Noise at the back of the screening room had him craning his neck to see who'd come in.

Jamey strode toward them looking completely awake, unlike Sierra. Although his coffee cup matched the enormous size of hers.

Rick was running on enough adrenaline right now as he waited to see if they'd pulled off movie magic last night. He hadn't needed anything more than a normal-sized cup and even that had his heart racing.

Jamey spotted Rick down near the front and waved, then worked his way between the rows to sit behind Rick. He leaned forward and rested his forearms on the back of Rick's seat.

"This is going to be fucking epic." The excitement was clear in Jamey's voice.

Rick blew out a puff of air. "We'd better hope it is."

Sierra cut him a sideways glance and gave a small nod. He didn't need the reminder that more than his future was on the line.

But more than just this movie was at stake here. Reputations followed stars from one movie to the next.

She loved him. He knew that. But could that love survive if he sank her career? That would change things. It would have to. And he wouldn't blame her if it did.

Shit.

But it had felt good last night. Of course that could have just been him thinking that because he missed that kind of action so damn much.

"All right. Let's get this show on the road."

Rick spun around again and saw that Howard had taken the first seat by the back door.

That felt like a bad sign. As if he wanted to be close to the exit so he could leave when the footage turned out to be so bad he couldn't stand watching it any longer.

Rick leaned closer to Sierra. "Does he always sit way back there?

She twisted to look, then glanced at Rick. "No."

Fuck.

The room was plunged into darkness until light from the projector illuminated the front of the screening room.

A test pattern flashed and then the wait was over. An image filled the screen. A wide shot of an inflatable rubber combat boat carrying eight men as it appeared on the horizon.

The SEALs from Coronado acted as the gunner on the automatic weapon at the bow and the coxswain controlling the tiller in the rear. The remaining six passengers in the lead boat, comprised of five more SEALs plus Jamey, leaned low and straddled the gunwale.

The second boat came into the shot. Both sped toward the shore and closer to the camera on the moonless night.

It was a hell of a sight to see, those two Zodiacs as they bounced over the water and raced toward the beach.

Next, a different camera zoomed in and provided a tight shot of Jamey, looking impressively like a SEAL right down to the expression of determined concentration on his face as his gaze stayed trained on the shore ahead.

The action continued as the sixteen-men leapt out of the Zodiacs and hit the beach running.

The combat-experienced operator in Rick studied every detail with a critical eye, searching for errors made by both the cast and the brand new SEALs fresh out of training.

He didn't find many. He didn't know if Howard would care about the precision with which they'd pulled this off, but Rick cared and it made him as proud as he was amazed.

Jamey did appear a little uncomfortable with the gun in his hands, not as natural as the SEALs looked with the weapons they carried, but the average movie goer wouldn't notice that. They'd be too enthralled with the action, not to mention the sound edits and music that would be added later.

Even as is, the raw footage looked totally kick ass. He couldn't help but smile as he reached out and squeezed Sierra's hand.

"This looks good. Right?" he asked, soft and close to her ear.

She cut her gaze sideways and nodded. "Yeah. It does."

Tempering his excitement, he focused his attention back to the screen.

Just because he and his girlfriend thought it was great didn't mean the director would. The verdict was still up in the air. But hell, at least he knew he'd tried his best and accomplished what he'd set out to do. The rest was up to Howard.

A flash of white on the screen caught his attention. There was a break in the footage and then a new scene replaced it. This one a shot of the interior of the island.

Rick saw a close-up of himself, laid out on his belly on the sand with a rifle. It was a position he'd held for hours—though not for as long as he would have had to in real combat. But the shoot had gone on long enough he'd eventually forgotten the cameras were there.

He certainly had no clue one was that close to him, zoomed in tight enough he could practically see the grease paint sunk into the individual pores of his skin.

The camera was on him as the explosives detonated on the beach. It caught his reaction as he rolled, leapt up and took off running. The shot followed him as he dove behind cover and fired his blanks at the supposed enemy.

It was odd watching himself, but he didn't have much time to consider that as the scene changed again. This time it focused on Jamey, lying on the ground, pretending pretty convincingly to be injured from the explosion.

Jamey's swollen face didn't matter now or for the scenes he'd been filming this week that were set in the hospital during his recovery.

He was good. The scene was dramatic. Convincing and eerily real looking as the SEAL from the graduating class dropped to his knees to tourniquet Jamey's fake leg wound.

Rick didn't know how much time passed. He was so enthralled by what was on screen. But finally the dailies ended. The screen went white again and the lights came up.

He glanced at Sierra. She didn't look sleepy anymore. Her eyes were wide open as she turned them toward him.

"Well?" he asked.

"Wow." Her single word gave him hope he was afraid to let himself feel.

He turned in his seat and saw Jamey. The kid's face broke into a wide smile. "Dude."

"You happy?" Rick asked.

"Happy?" Jamey shook his head. "I'm ecstatic. Holy shit, if this movie doesn't get nominated for a fuck ton of awards I'm quitting this business."

Great. No pressure there.

But there was still one person in the room who would determine the future of this movie, and his name wasn't Oscar.

Rick swallowed and dared to glance toward the back of the screening room.

Howard sat, still staring at the blank screen, eyes narrowed as if thinking, or maybe picturing the film after it had been edited?

Rick didn't know how Hollywood directors thought or operated. Hell, the only thing he knew was that Howard had better have liked what he saw or they were screwed.

Howard's gaze landed on Rick before he stood, drew his cell out of his pocket and headed out the door.

"What the fuck?" Eyes wide, Rick looked from Sierra to Jamey. "He left. What does that mean? Did he hate it?"

Sierra cringed as she shrugged. "I don't know."

"Fuck." Rick was about to lose his mind—and possibly his job. That didn't stop him.

Knocking against chairs, he took off up the aisle and out into the sunlight. He spotted Howard ahead of him, walking toward the production office.

Rick sprinted and caught up with him easily enough. He passed him and stopped, blocking his way.

Brows high, Howard said into the phone, "I'll call you back." He lowered the cell and tipped his head as he leveled a stare on Rick. "Yes?"

Now that he had the man's full attention, Rick wasn't sure he wanted it. He swallowed and steeled his nerve. "I need to know what you thought."

"Need to?" Howard smiled but not exactly in a jovial way. "You've got balls. You know that?"

"Yes, sir."

Howard shook his head. "You get away with all kinds of shit by following it up with that *sir*, don't you?"

"Not always," Rick confessed.

Howard outright laughed. "Honesty. I like that about you." He drew in a breath and let it out. "And I liked what I saw in there."

Rick's eyes widened. "You did?"

"Yes. It's good. It's real. It's raw and primal. Those might end up being the best scenes of this damn film, and that includes the ones of your girlfriend rolling around naked with Jamey."

Rick pressed his lips together as he moved past the allusion to the sex scenes and on to the important part of what Howard had said. He liked it.

"Thank you."

"You're welcome. But don't let it go to your head. You do anything to endanger or delay this production again and you'll be outside that gate looking in so fast your head will spin."

Rick couldn't help but smile. "Yes, sir. Understood."

Howard moved to step around Rick and then stopped. "Oh, and one more thing."

"Yeah?"

"You're not too bad in front of the camera. Might be something you want to consider."

Howard headed toward the office leaving Rick behind.

He was still standing there, flabbergasted,

watching him go when Sierra and Jamey arrived.

"What did he say?" Sierra's concern was clear.

Rick couldn't blame her for being worried. Hell, he'd been worried himself.

Luckily he could end her worry and Jamey's. "He loved it."

"Woo! Yeah!" Jamey punched a fist into the air. "I knew it. I'm gonna go talk to him."

As he took off in a sprint after Howard, Sierra smiled. "Congratulations."

"Thanks." Rick drew in and let out a breath now that his chest didn't feel like a two hundred and fifty pound weight was on it. "We should probably go home and get some sleep, but I think I'm too keyed up."

"I can't leave anyway. Howard rearranged the call sheet. I'm shooting a scene with just me today, no Jamey. So we don't fall behind."

"Shit. Okay. I'll stay here with you."

"No. You should go home and get some sleep. You're shooting on the island again tonight. Probably all night. You need your rest."

He let out a laugh. "I've gone without sleep before."

"Yes. But you had to then. You don't have to now."

He did have that list of bodyguards Jon had sent him just in case their plan didn't work out and he got kicked off the lot. One of them could stay with

Sierra for the day and escort her safely back to the hotel this evening.

Finally, he nodded. "All right. But only if you go home right after you're done here today and get some sleep. You can't be up all night and then work all day again."

She pressed her lips tight. "Okay."

"Good. It's a deal then." He leaned in and pressed a kiss to her lips. "Come on. I'll walk you to your trailer."

"Or the makeup trailer. Jeannie will have her work cut out for her covering the dark circles under my eyes today."

He shook his head. "You're still the most gorgeous woman on this lot."

"And you're delusional. A mixture of lack of sleep and the high you're riding because those scenes were amazing."

He grinned. "Yeah, they were. I've gotta call Jon and Zane and tell them. Those SEALs kicked ass last night."

"You miss it."

"Miss what?" He glanced down at her as they walked in the early morning sunlight.

"The action. The camaraderie. The excitement."

"Nah." He shook his head. "Last night was just fun. That's all."

"I don't know. I've never seen you in such a good mood. Well, maybe once."

"Oh really. And when was that?" The first time

they'd had sex, probably. That had been a pretty amazing day.

"That day I came to see you in the hospital right after you'd been shot. You were surrounded by your SEAL friends then too, all telling stories and reliving the past."

He lifted a shoulder. "That's what we do. Tell stories and relive the past. Doesn't mean I want to go back and do it all again."

"Don't you?" she asked, looking far too serious for such a great morning.

He stopped walking. Confused, he turned to face her, taking both of her hands in his. "What's this all about?"

She lifted a shoulder. "I don't know. It's nothing. Let me get to make-up so I can go to work and you can get some sleep."

He studied her for a second. This didn't feel resolved but she was right, they both had other things they should be doing.

More than that, after seeing those dailies and the discussion with Howard, he was in too good of a mood to let this odd discussion get him down.

CHAPTER THIRTEEN

It was another long night of shooting, but Rick was as hyped up as if he'd downed a case of energy drinks.

There was something about the action. About being part of a team. Even if he was working with new guys tonight instead of his old friends, he'd still loved every minute of it.

He hadn't realized how much he missed it all until now after getting a small taste of it again.

But he missed more than just being part of any team. He missed *his* team. *His* friends.

There was something he could do about that. Rick pulled out his cell phone and hit the contact listing for Jon.

Yeah, it was crazy early in the morning

California time, but it was a decent hour on the east coast, and it would be during normal working hours if Jon and Zane were still overseas.

Jon picked up after a couple of rings. "Hey, it's Mr. Hollywood. How are things going there?"

"Oh my God, dude. Everything went fucking perfect. It couldn't have been better."

"Really?" Jon laughed. "Well, that hardly ever happens."

"I know!" Rick laughed too. "But I swear, it was like clockwork. The FNGs were great. Jamey was great. Hell, a couple of people even said I was great."

"You, huh? They let you be in the movie? They must have really been desperate for warm bodies."

"Fuck you. And yeah, they were." Rick smiled, shaking his head at the teasing.

"Seriously though, I'm happy it all worked out."

"Yeah, me too. Thank you, and thank Zane too. For everything."

"You can thank Zane yourself. He'll be back out in Cali in a couple of weeks."

"Good. I'll have to take him out for a drink. And what about you? Where are you at right now?" Rick never knew where Jon might be when he answered the phone.

It could be anywhere from Detroit to Djibouti, knowing how widespread their business was.

"Zane and I had a whirlwind forty-eight hours in HOA, but I'm home again. For now."

When he'd been tied to his boring guard job at the nuclear reactor in Virginia, he used to be envious of all their travel. Now that he lived out of hotel rooms half the year, he was definitely over it.

Jon could have his whirlwind trips to the Horn of Africa. Rick had finally learned to appreciate the pleasures of being home. He was sure Jon felt the same now he had a wife and kid.

"That's good to hear, bud. I'm sure Ali appreciates having you home . . . you know, to help change poopy diapers." Rick chuckled.

"Yeah." Jon let out a snort. "Thanks for the reminder. I've gotta take out the trash. It's getting a bit aromatic thanks to those diapers. And I gotta mow the lawn before it rains. And run out to the store and pick up some milk because we're out."

Hearing Jon talk made daily housekeeping and room service seem a whole lot better. Rick appreciated hotel life a little more after Jon's To Do list. Perhaps he didn't hate living in hotels and short-term rentals wherever Sierra was filming as much as he thought.

Rick smiled. "That's a hell of a list. I'll let you go get to it. I just wanted to give you an update and say thanks for the help."

"No problem. It was fun. I'm glad it all worked out for you . . . and just so you know, I expect two tickets to the premiere."

"You got it." Rick smiled, and then sobered as he realized it could easily be months before he saw his friend again. "Miss you, dude."

"Miss you too, brother. Say hi to Sierra for me."

"You too—say hey to Ali. Talk to you soon."

"You got it." Jon disconnected and Rick pocketed his cell.

Yeah, he missed the guys, but there was something else he was missing just as much right now, if not more. Crawling into bed beside Sierra.

He slipped the hotel room keycard out of its slot in his wallet and shoved it into the door lock. The light turned from red to green—his invitation inside after a long night.

In fact, it had been two long nights, but now it was time for bed and sleep . . . and hopefully more than sleep when they both woke tomorrow. Or rather, later today since it was well past midnight and creeping closer to dawn.

He'd ridden the bus back to the lot with the crew and showered there, so in the suite he dumped his duffle bag on the floor inside the door and headed straight for the bedroom.

She'd left the living room light on but the bedroom was dark, except for the strip of light coming in from the open doorway between the two rooms, but he knew this room well enough by now to navigate his way to the bed in the darkness.

His weight jostled her on the mattress. He heard her draw in a deep breath and let in out on a moan. The sound had him getting hard immediately.

"You're back," she said, sounding sleepy.

"I am." He slipped between the sheets and

moved across the sprawling king-sized mattress toward her side of the bed.

"Good." Sierra was on top of him before he even had a chance to reach for her, straddling him and his happy erection.

He palmed her ass and found she had nothing on beneath the short nightie she wore. "Whoa. Not that I'm complaining, but what brought this on?"

"I don't know," she said as she captured his face between her hands and moved in for a tongue-deep kiss.

When she broke for air, he said, "Damn. Something got into you. Tell me."

"I don't know. I had a good day on the set today. And I guess seeing you all SEALed out like that in the dailies this morning got to me."

"Oh, did it?" He grinned.

She backhanded him in the arm. "Don't sound so cocky about it."

"Oh, I'm definitely feeling cocky." He laughed knowing she could feel the very obviously aroused appendage beneath her.

They hadn't done this in days. Not since that fateful night he'd lost his cool and punched Jamey.

He'd started to worry he'd done irreparable damage to their relationship. Sex wasn't everything. It was nothing to base a relationship on, but it sure sucked when it was missing from theirs.

Who knew all it took was some war games and greasepaint to get his woman excited? He'd have to remember that.

Maybe they should take up paintball together or go to the gun range.

That was something to consider later. Much later. After he'd gotten back to where he needed to be. Inside her.

She squeaked as he used his own legs to spread hers wide. He'd have many more and varied sounds coming out of her shortly.

Just the thought had him groaning as he slid down her legs.

No doubt she knew what was coming. She'd argue with him over just about anything, always had and he suspected always would, but she wasn't fighting him now.

Oh no. Instead she spread her legs farther apart to allow room for the width of his shoulders between them.

Rick slipped his arms under her thighs. With one palm beneath each of her ass cheeks, he raised her core to meet his mouth.

He reveled in her reaction as she threw her head back against the pillow and moaned with pleasure. Real pleasure, not the pretend movie kind. And he'd done it to her.

Pride filled him as he worked her into an orgasm before he slid up her body and thrust inside her. He took his own pleasure, allowing himself to follow her quickly down the path to orgasm.

He needed the release too badly to deny himself. Needed just as much to lay that claim on her body after the wedge he'd put between them recently.

His eyes had adjusted to the dimness in the bedroom and he could see well enough to appreciate her sated expression.

He'd never grow tired of staring down at this woman beneath him. Never weary of hearing her gasp from his touch.

She was it—the one for him. He'd felt it for a while but here and now it was clear as day. There was no doubt. He wanted to live and die loving this woman.

Until death do them part.

It was huge—thinking those words and what they meant—but not frightening. He'd never been more sure of anything before in his life.

But damn that was too serious a subject for him to tackle now.

Time for some lighter conversation . . . like how she'd gotten excited watching the dailies. That would serve as a good distraction from the serious turn his brain had taken.

If he knew one thing it was that Sierra expected—and deserved—a proposal worthy of a fairy tale. Blurting out *will you marry me* while his cock was still inside her wasn't going to cut it, no matter how hyped up he felt.

Rolling over, Rick reached for the bedside lamp and turned it on so he could better see his woman.

There was nothing prettier than the post-climatic pink glow in the cheeks of a lady well satisfied.

That was part of the reason for his smile, but not the whole reason.

Her sudden attraction to his SEAL past was . . . "So seeing me all *SEALed out*, as you put it, got you going. Huh?"

"Yes." She rolled her eyes. "I'm going to regret telling you that, aren't I?"

"No. Not at all." He hoped he could keep that promise as he said, "I just never pegged you as a frog hog."

"I don't even know what that is but I really do not like the sound of it."

He laughed. "Just teasing you, princess."

"Don't tease. I'm being serious. I mean I know what you used to do in the Navy, but I never got to see you in action."

"Not true. I do believe we were shot at on the movie lot in Virginia. That was certainly some action."

"Yeah, but you weren't in all the accessories and stuff."

That elicited a belly laugh. "Are you calling my body armor and rifle *accessories*, woman?" he asked.

"If the word fits." She shrugged. "And the makeup too. I really liked you in the makeup."

"Jesus." Rick ran his hand over his face.

Her calling the camo greasepaint *makeup* was the last straw. He rolled on top of her before she completely emasculated him and he couldn't perform.

Although judging by the renewed rock-hard length between his legs, that wasn't going to be a problem.

"Again?" she asked, smiling as she teased.

It was an easy answer to give. "Again, and again, and again. Always."

CHAPTER FOURTEEN

"Did you see those dailies?" Jamey was so excited he was glowing, and it wasn't just from the yellow hue of his ever changing bruise.

"Yes, I did see." Sierra smiled, indulging him since she'd been seated between him and Rick in the screening room so he knew she'd seen them.

He rolled his eyes. "I know I'm being ridiculous getting so excited over dailies, but they were great, right? I mean I haven't been in as many movies as you have. You're like here . . ." Jamey raised his arm high above his head, and then lowered it and continued, "And I'm way down here. I know that, but what we're seeing is still good, right?"

She nodded. "Yeah. It's good."

Rick and the SEALs he'd somehow borrowed

from the Navy had killed it. Last night's scenes were even better than the first night's.

She couldn't deny it, not that she wanted to. What was good for the movie was good for everyone involved in it.

Jamey was smiling again, satisfied she'd agreed with him. "That means a lot that you think it's good too. I mean you've been in this business forever."

Sierra pressed her lips together. *Forever.* Yeah. That didn't make her feel old at all. "It sure feels that way."

As they walked outside across the lot, Jamey cut his gaze sideways to her. "Did I ever tell you? The first movie I ever saw, I mean the first real adult one out at the theater, was yours."

"No, you never told me." She had a feeling the rest of this story wasn't going to go well. At least not well for her or her insecurity.

"I wasn't old enough to see it because it was rated R. So my friend got his older brother to buy the tickets for us and we slipped in behind an older couple, you know, pretending like they were our mom and dad." He grinned wide. "And now we're starring together."

"We are." But for how much longer would they continue to cast her as the love interest when the hero was a decade younger than she was?

Not long was her guess. She could buy herself a few more years with enough Botox and line fillers, maybe a little collagen in her lips and the right hairstyle, but that wouldn't work forever.

Soon she'd start to get roles as the star's mother. Or worse, grandmother.

Hollywood was a real bastard and the viewing public its fickle mistress. Which is why it was important to strike while the iron was still hot. Before her career cooled to the point she'd have to take action to keep it on life support.

Deciding to move on from the gloomy future she'd envisioned, she glanced at Jamey. "Your swelling is way down."

He nodded. "You see that? I thought so too. Now it's just the bruise."

"And Jeannie can cover that no problem."

"Exactly. Today's scenes should be fine. I think we're in the clear."

They were scheduled to shoot another flashback scene. This one depicting when she and Jamey first saw each other after he gets back from deployment.

"Howard wouldn't have scheduled them if he didn't think so," Sierra agreed.

"What happened really is a blessing."

She frowned and shot him a glance. "How's that?"

"If Rick didn't punch me, we never would have had to rearrange the schedule to shoot the flashbacks earlier. We would have shot it as planned and that wasn't with the real SEALs and all their kick ass military shit."

"You're correct there."

Jamey shook his head. "Rick really is amazing."

Sierra smiled. The hero worship in this *bromance* was starting to reach a comedic level. "Yup. Amazing."

"You two have been together a while."

"A couple of years." She nodded.

"That's forever in Hollywood." He grinned.

She laughed. "We spent a considerable amout of that time on the east coast. I have a house in Miami and was working on a film shooting in Virginia when we met."

He nodded, as if that explained the longevity of the relationship.

"How come you're not dating?" she asked.

The hottest new actor to hit the big screen in years should have at least the rumor of a girlfriend, if not a sex tape making the rounds on the internet by now.

He let out a snort. "Who has the time?"

She laughed. "True."

"Maybe I should date Jeannie. I see her more than any other woman in my life besides you."

Sierra noticed Jamey hadn't suggested they date. She chose to assume that was because she was with Rick and not because she was too old to be in his dating pool, while the twenty-something Jeannie was right there in the zone.

She knew he was just making a joke but she figured he should know the deal anyway. "I think Jeannie's girlfriend might take issue with you two dating."

His eyes widened as he turned to stare at her. "No!"

"Yes." Sierra laughed.

"Wow." And with that Jamey's horny male mind was no doubt filled with lesbian fantasies.

Sierra shook her head. God bless 'em, the men in her life were so predictable.

And speaking of the men in her life . . . Rick came trotting up to them. "Hey, you'll never guess what Howard wanted to talk to me about when he pulled me away after the screening."

"Um, I probably never will guess so why don't you tell us?" she said.

"He wants me to do press with you."

"Well, you're my security so you of course will be traveling with me—"

Rick shaking his head interrupted her. "No. He wants me on camera."

Maybe the men in her life weren't as predictable as she'd assumed.

"On camera?" she asked.

"Yeah. He's trying to set up some sort of promo shoot at Coronado for Jamey and me," Rick continued, looking as excited as Jamey.

Jamey's mouth dropped open. "Holy shit. For real? I get to go to the base where the SEALs train, with you?"

"Yup." Rick nodded. "You even get to run the

obstacle course."

"The one you run in BUD/S? No way!" Jamey's eyes popped wide.

The two were like boys on Christmas morning. And what did that make her?

Right now she felt suspiciously like their mommy.

They walked off ahead, Rick as animated as Jamey as they talked.

He loved this shit. Absolutely and completely.

But what happened when there were no more SEAL scenes to shoot? No more promos on Navy bases to do? What then?

When it was back to hours of non-eventful boring old guard duty, Rick was going to be more miserable than he had been before.

He might not be able to see that far ahead but she could and she dreaded that day.

She didn't want to think about it but she had to, because it wasn't all that far away.

CHAPTER FIFTEEN

Coronado. This was the place where SEALs were made. It was also where many a candidate's dreams were crushed.

Rick stood on the grinder.

The place where he'd stood so many years ago and gotten his trident at graduation. The place he'd mustered daily regardless of heat or rain or cold. The place where he'd dropped and gave the instructors as many push-ups as it took to make them happy.

The infamous brass bell where so many candidates had rung out, giving up when things had gotten too tough, was located purposefully within sight of the grinder where so much activity happened.

He saw the small sign that spelled out the dose of cold hard truth they'd all lived during that period—*the only easy day was yesterday*.

It was almost impossible to absorb all the things assaulting him at once. Sights. Sounds. Smells. Memories.

"You miss this," Sierra said next to him.

"This?" Rick laughed, sweeping a hand to indicate their surroundings. "No." He looked over at Sierra and saw the doubt in her expression. "I promise you, there is nothing about BUD/S that I miss."

Not the sleep deprivation. Not the sugar cookies. Not the drown proofing. Not the master chief's shouting.

He saw a class run by. A tight formation full of energized candidates who answered the cadence loud and clear, proving this was just the beginning of their training day and not near the end.

Okay, maybe he did miss that. Not the miles of running, but rather the camaraderie. The feeling of being part of a team. Part of a group with a shared purpose, all dedicated to something bigger than themselves.

He glanced again at Sierra and saw her still watching him.

She'd been doing that a lot lately—watching him. In fact, it had been happening since they'd shot those night scenes. That was over a month ago now.

He had the distinct feeling she was waiting for something. For what, he didn't know. Maybe for him to lose his cool again and punch somebody?

If that were the case she needn't have worried. If he ever did punch Jamey again, it would because the kid was so close up his ass every moment that Rick couldn't stop without Jamey running into the back of him.

The only reason he wasn't here with them now was because he was getting his makeup put on for today's promo shoot.

Yeah, Rick understood the importance of makeup for actors in the movies, but for running the O-course? Ridiculous.

Needless to say Rick had refused the offer. He didn't care what Jeannie said about the camera and the sunlight washing him out.

That's all he needed, makeup mixed with the sweat running into his eyes and the sand blowing in his face while he tried to cross Burma Bridge on the obstacle course. No, thank you.

"Come on." He reached for and grabbed Sierra's hand.

"Where are we going?" she asked.

"To the beach."

Hopefully there'd be a BUD/S class there doing something torturous. Rolling in the surf in full uniform. Carrying one of those heavy ass logs he'd had to for hours at a time. Running with a boat held over their heads.

Any of those things would show Sierra he wasn't lying about not missing his time at Coronado before he'd gotten assigned to an east coast team and from there moved on to DEVGRU.

Although, maybe it didn't matter if she never did truly understand. That part of his life was over now.

They didn't get even as far as the sand when Jamey trotted up to them. With him came a cameraman, a sound guy and assorted other crew whose purpose Rick had yet to figure out.

"Hey! Ready for the obstacle course?" Jamey asked.

Sierra looked relieved to be saved from the long trek across the sand Rick had proposed. She was such a city girl.

Rick turned his attention to Jamey, who was practically vibrating with excitement.

"Sure," Rick said. "Are *you* ready?"

"Hell, yeah!" Jamey rubbed his hands together. "I can't wait."

Rick laughed, sure the kid's tune would change at about the third obstacle. "Okay. Let's hit it. We can walk over." He paused and glanced down at Sierra's impractical heels, then took a look at all the crew and their equipment. "Or maybe we should drive over."

Alone, he never would have thought twice about heading to the O-course on foot. Today, he was definitely not alone.

They drove the short way to the obstacle course set up on the sand and everyone piled out of the vehicles.

Rick waited next to Jamey as the crew got their shit together. "So I'll go first so you can see the procedure. Then I'll walk alongside you while you go through it. Okay?"

"Okay. Got it. Let's do this."

Rick looked forward to seeing what happened to all that enthusiasm later, after Jamey had faced the infamous course.

"All righty." Rick slipped off his sunglasses and took his cell phone out of one of the pockets of his camouflage pants—a remnant of his active-duty past. He handed both to Sierra. "Hold these for me?"

"Sure." As she took the items, he could see even through the lenses of her sunglasses that her gaze swept him from head to toe.

Was she checking him out? His lips twitched with a smile. He was going to have to start wearing cammies more often if that was all it took to get Sierra's motor running.

He delivered a wink. "See you in a few minutes."

With Jamey standing next to him at the course's start looking excited, Rick asked, "You gonna time me?"

It wasn't being able to just finish the course that was important. Candidates were judged by how fast they could complete it.

Jamey stared blankly at Rick.

"I got you." Jeannie, the make-up girl of all

people, held up her cell phone to show Rick the timer app was open. "Whenever you're ready."

At the moment, he trusted Jeannie to remember to hit start on the timer more than Jamey in his excited state, so Rick nodded.

He drew in a breath and took off for the first obstacle.

It was the tires. A piece of cake, but that was part of the challenge. The course started out deceptively easy and got hella hard fast.

He navigated the tires easily and jumped right into the parallel bars for the Hand Walk.

It had been years since he'd been here and run this course, but it came right back to him. He'd run it so often as a candidate his muscles remembered what to do. He ran it without having to think.

As he moved from one obstacle to the next—the low wall, then the rope climb up and over the high wall—he was aware of the crowd of people following along beside him.

He was used to being watched on the course, they were tested and timed on it weekly during training, but then the people with him were instructors, a medic and other candidates. Not a film crew. But as he executed a practiced belly crawl beneath the logs that were to simulate barbed wire, he really didn't care who watched him. His eye was on his end goal—a good completion time.

He climbed up the cargo net and back down again.

Balancing on the rolling logs felt easier than it

used to and a small part of his brain wondered if that was because his balance had improved thanks to his taking up surfing.

He conquered getting over the logs that made up the Dirty Name and the tightrope of Burma Bridge as easily as if he'd done this course just last month. He moved smoothly through the Weaver, lacing his body over and under the metal bars.

By the time he reached the vaults he knew he was in the final stretch and poured on the speed.

Sprinting, he reached the sign to indicate the finish line and yelled, "Time!"

Bent at the waist and breathing hard, Rick braced his hands on his thighs and glanced up at Jeannie.

"Nine minutes."

"What?" He straightened, his chest still heaving as he tried to catch his breath. "Are you sure?"

"Yeah. Well actually, eight minutes and forty-nine seconds."

He blew out a curse. Eight minutes and change sounded moderately better than nine, but still, it was way slower than what he'd used to get.

Gone were the days of a six-minute completion time for him. Well over a decade of years passing and a couple of knee surgeries did that to a guy, he supposed.

Jamey trotted up to him. "Oh my God. That was amazing. You made it look so easy."

He let out a breathy laugh. *Easy* was not a word

he'd use to describe the O-course.

"You ready?" Rick asked.

"Yeah." Jamey nodded.

Time to kick some civilian ass to make himself feel better about his own time. "All right. Let's get back to the start."

The presence of the film crew had attracted a few on-lookers. Guys in brown shirts and cammies, which told Rick they were candidates.

They probably had intended on doing a practice run on the course but found the whole Hollywood circus set up down here on the sand instead.

When he glanced behind him and found Sierra signing an autograph for one guy, he guessed they didn't mind the interruption in their workout all that much.

But back to Jamey. He needed to make sure the kid didn't die or break anything. They still had some shit to do to tie up this movie, not to mention the whole press tour and publicity stuff.

That was the very reason they were here today. To show the viewing public all the real life military background that had gone into the making of this completely fictional film.

He supposed the public would appreciate it. Or maybe not. What did he know? He wasn't an expert in movies or publicity.

What he was an expert on was this course.

"Take your time as you go through," Rick said. "Don't burn yourself out by trying to sprint in between. Running in the sand is exhausting and you need your strength for the obstacles."

He was talking but he wasn't sure Jamey was listening. The kid was in a sprinter's stance at the starting line, looking like he was ready to take off for the fifty-yard dash.

He would learn soon enough. Rick glanced at Jeannie. "Got the timer ready?"

"Yup." She nodded. "I'm ready."

Short of having a starter's gun, Rick figured Jamey needed some sort of official go-ahead, so he said, "All right, Jamey. Ready. Set. Go!"

The kid took off running, doing just as Rick had told him not to do.

He almost tripped on the tires by trying to take them too fast but he made it through without face planting, which was good.

Rick had already seen the results of Pretty Boy having a messed up face. He didn't need a repeat of that.

The kid jumped easily over the first wall. No surprise. He was tall and at this point in the course, was still fresh and full of energy.

That wasn't going to last.

"Save yourself in between," Rick yelled.

Jamey climbed the wall with the rope easily as well. That obstacle was all about upper body strength, and whether his muscles were more for show or for actual use, Rick had to admit Jamey had good upper body definition.

Maybe he wasn't going to do as badly on this course as Rick had predicted. His ego was starting to feel bruised until the kid executed the slowest belly crawl Rick had ever seen.

That was one of the easier stations in the course, as far as Rick was concerned. Although he supposed civilians didn't practice crawling under barbed wire so perhaps it was an acquired skill.

As Jamey ran toward the Cargo Net, Rick remembered his coaching duties. "Stay close to the side on the way up. The rope's tighter there."

Jamey jumped onto the rope and started to climb.

"Stop at the mid point where it's marked in red. We can only go halfway up without a medic present since you can die if you fall from the top."

That got Jamey's attention. He paused in his climb and glanced down at Rick, eyes wide.

So the kid *was* listening.

Rick smiled. "Don't stop now. Get up and get back down. Clock's ticking."

Jamey managed it without falling off, though it wasn't the fastest climb Rick had ever seen.

He moved toward the board walking, slipping off as one of the logs rolled when he stepped on it.

"Start over," Rick yelled.

"From the beginning?" Jamey gasped.

"No. On the log."

"Oh." Jamey blew out a breath and this time took the logs much slower, balancing with his arms extended.

"You do any surfing?" Rick asked him.

"No," Jamey answered, already sounding breathless.

"Too bad. I think it helps with the board walking."

Jamey scowled, almost fell off the last log, but finally made it to the end. Finally learning, or maybe just tiring, he walked rather than ran to the rope climb.

"Jump as high as you can to start. That way you have less climbing to do," Rick called to him.

The kid was getting tired. He climbed a lot more slowly than he had the rope wall, but managed to get up, swing across to the second rope and climb down again without falling.

Meanwhile the group watching them was growing. Rick did his best to ignore the on-lookers. At least they hadn't all been here for his less than optimal run.

He couldn't be concerned with that now because Jamey had reached the Dirty Name.

It was set up like the uneven bars in gymnastics, but since these were logs, not bars, they were impossible to grab with just your hands.

"Just jump and hook one arm and one leg over the high log," Rick said.

Jamey shot him a look. "Are you nuts?"

Rick laughed. "No. I did it."

"Yeah, you did. It looked easier when you were up here."

"Just give it a try. You have three attempts before you have to move on."

Jamey drew in a breath and finally nodded, leaping at the high horizontal log and catching it with both hands before he slipped off.

"That's one."

Grumbling, Jamey went back to the first log, jumped up onto it and eyed the high log. He leapt at it, this time getting one arm and almost getting his torso over before he slipped off.

"That's two," Rick said, knowing he was being annoying and enjoying it as Jamey got more frustrated.

Jamey's grumbled obscenities had Rick chuckling. This obstacle was called the Dirty Name for a reason.

Finally, he leapt and did what Rick said. He managed to hook one leg and arm over the log before he wiggled his whole body over and dropped to the ground.

"Good. That only cost you like four minutes."

Stumbling across the sand, Jamey scowled again, but after the challenge of the Dirty Name, the rest of the course didn't present as many difficulties.

The rest of his run was slow and messy.

After a faulty start on the Weaver where he had to figure out how to make it over and under while still holding on, Jamey made it through the metal bars.

He climbed up and made it across the rope Burma Bridge and finally figured out his hand and foot holds on the Traverse Wall. He shimmied across the low rope upside down. Managed another balance walk without falling off the logs and did the Monkey Bars fairly quickly, if a little sloppy.

By the vaults, Jamey was throwing his body over the logs and stumbled to the finish.

Rick yelled, "Time!" He glanced at Jeannie. "How long?"

She cringed. "Nineteen minutes and thirty-two seconds."

"What?" His whole body heaving as he tried to catch his breath, Jamey managed to get the single word out.

Rick shook his head. "Dude, that's really not bad."

Jamey screwed up his mouth. "It's not good."

Rick laughed. "It was your first time. Give yourself a break. There are some guys who wouldn't even be able to finish."

"Really?" Jamey asked.

"Yes, really. There's a rumor—I don't know if it's true or not—that Lance Armstrong, the bike dude, got stuck on top of the cargo net. Froze from fear and they had to get him down."

"For real? Wow." That seemed to appease Jamey.

"You did good. A little practice and you'd have no problem."

"You're not just saying that?" Jamey asked Rick.

"I promise." Rick turned and almost ran into the cameraman, still right there in his face. They'd run the course, so what was the camera guy waiting for?

"We done here?" Rick asked him, knowing he probably shouldn't be talking directly to the camera.

"I don't know. You doing anything else?" the camera guy asked.

Rick lifted a brow. "We only have permission to film the O-course, so I'd say that's a no to doing anything else."

"All righty." Finally, the cameraman flipped a switch and the red light blinked off.

Relieved, Rick turned back to Jamey. "Drink some water so you don't dehydrate. And clean out those cuts on your hands and arms."

Jamey glanced down as if noticing for the first time the red raw streaks on his skin before looking back up at Rick. "You're a real good coach. You should teach here or something."

Sierra had made her way across the sand to them. She handed Rick his cell and glasses and said, "He's right. Did you ever think about teaching the new guys?"

"Be an instructor?" Rick laughed. "Yeah, no. My active duty days are over. My old commander, Grant Milton, actually did that for a little while—

became a Green Team instructor. He didn't love it. He missed the action and ended up going back to the team after a year."

There was that look again. Sierra's gaze seemed to penetrate deep into him, evaluating his words and the truth behind them.

He'd gladly stare into those eyes of hers for hours—particularly while they were in bed—but this felt different.

Something was definitely up with her. He reached out and pulled her close, pressing a kiss to her forehead.

"Ready to head out?" he asked, deciding what he needed was some time alone with her to get over this weirdness.

"Yeah, sure." She nodded.

"Good. Let's go."

She had something on her mind and as soon as they wrapped up this damn promotional shit for this film, he intended to get to the bottom of it and find and what.

CHAPTER SIXTEEN

They were back at the hotel, but Sierra couldn't get the obstacle course at Coronado off her mind.

It had been eye opening, watching Rick run that course.

He was smooth and fast and strong. So comfortable, like it was second nature to him to be hanging from nets thirty feet in the air, or running across rope bridges.

Sierra supposed it was second nature to him. It had been how he'd lived for more than half of his adult life.

Now his life was completely different . . . and she wasn't sure how he felt about it. Or how she felt about it either.

He had been in his element during the shoot on

the beach. From when he'd planned that scene with his old teammates. To when he'd organized the SEALs they'd brought in as extras for the scene. He loved every minute of it. She could see that.

Whether he was joking one minute or completely serious the next, he was right where he was supposed to be—in the middle of the action.

His demeanor during that shoot, and again at the base today, was the opposite of the stone-faced, tight-jawed version of the man who was her head of security. The man she'd become used to these past couple of years.

It was obvious. He needed the action. Needed to lead a team.

He hadn't been doing that for the past few years and that was because of her. She'd plucked him right out of the environment where he'd belonged— working with his teammates for a company that sent men like Rick around the globe to protect the world from everything bad.

She'd separated him from the friends he loved and from his life's purpose and stuck him in the role of her bodyguard.

No wonder he was so sullen. He was bored. Here he worked alone. There was no challenge. No purpose.

Rick had gone from literally saving the world to standing around for eighteen hours a day on the off chance someone got too close to her.

He'd gone from going full out, giving one hundred and ten percent at all times, living on adrenaline, to now throttling all that energy inside him.

She'd seen the results of that. He'd lost his cool and had broken Jamey's cheekbone with one punch.

Rick stayed with her and did a job he was overqualified for and bored with because he loved her.

He did it because just once in her acting career a psycho had become a threat and nearly did her harm. Rick had saved her back then and he was determined to save her now.

Rick had put himself in charge of making sure it never happened again . . . and it was making his life miserable.

It was clear what she had to do. She had to put his well being above her own. She had to do the hardest thing she'd ever had to do, for his sake.

She needed to let him go.

"Hey." At the sound of his voice, Sierra glanced up to see Rick watching her. "You okay?"

"Uh." She swallowed. "Yeah."

He frowned. "You sure?"

"Yeah. Fine." As fine as she could be. "So, it was nice seeing Jon and Zane, wasn't it?"

He frowned but nodded. "Yeah. It was."

"Maybe you should take a trip to Virginia for a little while now that the filming is done," she suggested.

"Yeah. That would be cool. How much time do we have before you start the next film?"

"A few months."

He nodded. "Okay, so after the press tour for this movie, let's plan on spending some time in Virginia."

"Or you could go now," she said.

Rick frowned. "But you're flying to New York to start the talk show circuit next week."

She lifted one shoulder, trying to look more casual than she felt. "Yeah, but I don't really need you there for that."

He looked at her as if she were crazy. "What do you mean? Why not?"

"I'll be with Jamey. I don't think anyone will bother me."

Rick drew back, his sandy brows drawn low over his eyes. "What's going on?"

"What do you mean? Nothing's going on. I just thought you might want to take some jobs with Jon and Zane's company, since you enjoy that work so much." It took all of her acting skills to play dumb.

If she could just get him to go back to his old life, he'd realize how much he missed it. Then maybe he'd make the choice to leave on his own.

Eyes on her, he said, "I *enjoy* being with you."

"Yeah, but you're really good at all the military stuff. Don't you want to put all that skill to good use?"

"I do put it to good use. By protecting you." His words were slow and measured.

"But you really seem like you're wasting your

training just being a bodyguard."

"Carey, what's really going on here?" he asked.

Uh oh. He'd used her real name. Things always felt a hundred times more serious—more real—when he did that.

She drew in a breath and let it out. "I think you shouldn't be in charge of my security anymore."

"Why not?" The tone of his voice rose with surprise.

"Because you need to go back to your old life."

Rick shook his head, obviously confused as he asked, "Why?"

"Because you were better there doing what you used to do than you are here."

He narrowed his eyes. "Is this because of what I did to Jamey?"

She bobbed her head. "Partially."

"I fixed that. It was a mistake. I apologized. I made it right. Howard and the studio are fine with how it turned out. Happy even."

"I'm not." She wasn't happy because the man she'd met in Virginia would never have punched a guy for no good reason. Would never have mistrusted her and believed she'd cheat on him.

That man had been confident and bold, but measured and calm. This man before her now was nothing like that.

Rick had changed. Being with her had changed him. It was time for her to make things right.

"Why are you doing this? Wait." His eyes widened. "Is it because I was in the movie? If that's it, I promise you I don't want to be in front of the camera ever again. I'm perfectly happy to let you be the one in the spotlight. You're the star. I just want to be there and keep you safe."

"It's not that. I know you're not interested in being on screen and even if you were, I wouldn't care. Jesus, Rick, my ego isn't that big."

He spread his hands wide, obviously at a loss. "Then what is it?"

"It's you. I've never seen you so happy as when you were in those dirty trenches, dressed in camo, running alongside those SEALs with a gun in your hand."

He lifted a shoulder. "Yeah, it was fun for a couple of nights running ops with the teams without anyone shooting at us for real."

She shook her head. "You wouldn't have cared even if they were shooting real bullets instead of blanks."

He opened his mouth to speak and she cut him off.

"You're miserable on set, Rick. I can see it. I don't want to be the person who puts that expression on your face."

"You're not. I'm happy just being with you."

"Happy men don't suspect their girlfriends of cheating on them and they don't beat the shit out of innocent men over it."

Looking up at the ceiling, Rick let out a huff

before focusing back on her. "I did everything I could do to make up for that."

"I know. It's not enough." She was being tough. It was the only way with him. She knew that.

"Fine. I'll arrange for someone else to take over your security."

"And go back to working for Jon and Zane?" she asked.

He sighed. "Yeah. I'll see what jobs they have out here in California. Or wherever your next movie shoot is going to be."

She shook her head. "No."

"What do you mean no?" He eyed her.

"You know the hours I work. We'll rarely see each other and when we're not together you'll be suspicious, wondering what I'm doing. Whom I'm with."

"One time! I know I was crazy suspecting you and Jamey. I know I was wrong. I apologized. I learned from my mistake."

"You can't change who you are at the core. I saw your face as you watched us together. You hated every minute I was with Jamey."

"It's your job. I understand that. I can handle it."

"No, you can't. You almost killed a major motion picture because you can't."

"I can—"

"No. Rick, you need a woman who's all yours. Not one who gets paid to be with other men. And that's fine. You should have that. But it can't be me."

Rick continued to frown, slowly shaking his head. "I don't want to break up over this."

"I don't see any other way." It tore her heart out to say it, but it was true.

If they stayed together, he'd end up ruining her career. She hated to admit it but this decision was as much for her sake as for his.

Things hadn't felt the same since that morning in Howard's office. Maybe she never did completely forgive Rick for suspecting her and Jamey. For punching him and putting the film in jeopardy.

Hell, maybe they just needed a break from each other to figure things out. She didn't know. All she knew was that as long as he stayed, things would remain the same. And the way things were wasn't working any longer. Something had to change.

"It's gotta be this way, Rick. I think a complete break will be easier for both of us."

"No. Carey . . ."

Tears pricked behind her eyes. She couldn't let him talk. If he did, he might say something to make her change her mind. "I'll book you a flight to Virginia for tomorrow morning. I'll get another room for myself for tonight."

Before he could try to stop her, she grabbed her purse and reached for the doorknob.

As she left she caught one last glimpse of Rick standing alone in the living room of suite.

The sight of his distraught expression and slumped shoulders was enough to break her heart, but it wasn't enough to make her stay.

CHAPTER SEVENTEEN

It had been too long since Rick had been home.

Six months, at least. Yet he noticed he still thought of this place—his sister's house where he only had a room to sleep in when he needed it—as home.

That probably should have told him something. Been a big old honking clue that something was wrong.

Looking back it sure was.

It said that the more than two years he'd spent with Sierra, traveling the world amid glitz and glamour, had been more of a fantasy than reality.

They'd never put down roots. Sure, she owned a place in Miami, but that was hers and they were rarely there anyway.

But he wasn't even concerned about the property ownership. Whose name was on the deed didn't matter. He wasn't that kind of guy who couldn't handle it when a woman earned more than he did.

How could he be? He'd gone into the military knowing what the salaries were. And the tabloids were very good at letting the world know what Sierra earned per movie and there was no way he could ever equal that stratospheric amount no matter how hard he worked.

The problem wasn't real estate or bank accounts. It was that they'd never created a home that was theirs together. A home base formed jointly from the two of them. Their combined hearts and souls. Interests and likes.

Perhaps that was a good thing. If they had, he'd be losing his home as well as his girlfriend.

Head hanging as heavily as his heart, Rick reached out and rang the doorbell.

He had his key, but this was Darci and Chris's place now.

Rick didn't feel right barging in on the married couple that was purportedly trying to conceive a baby. He didn't need to walk in on that scene. He had enough weighing on him as it was.

The front door swung wide and the looming figure that was his old teammate and new brother-in-law filled the opening.

"Well, I'll be damned. Come on in." Chris's southern hospitality welcomed Rick into what had been his own home. As Chris closed the door with them both inside, he said, "I didn't know you were fixin' to visit."

Unfortunately, this wasn't a visit. Rick should probably tell him that. "Um—"

"Rick. Did I miss a text from you that you were coming?" Darci asked from the kitchen. Her gaze cut to Chris. "I told you that cheap cell phone service you switched us to was no good."

Rick held up his hand before his presence created marital discord. "No. I didn't text. I'm sure your cell phone is just fine."

Chris might talk slow, but his mind was sharp as a tack. He watched Rick through narrowed eyes as he asked, "What's wrong?"

All right. This was it. Rick drew in a deep breath and said, "We broke up."

Three little words. Not the three he wanted to be saying.

He would have far rather told them he'd come home to grab his grandmother's ring. The one he kept stashed in a box in the corner of his gun safe here at the house.

Unfortunately, today's three little words were not *I'm getting married*. He only wished they were.

Darci reacted about as expected. Quick and loud and with a lot of questions.

Chris's only reaction was a slight lift of a brow, and then he was on his way to the liquor cabinet. Without asking he bent and grabbed a bottle from inside. He planted it on the coffee table on his way to the kitchen cabinet where he grabbed two short glasses.

Yeah. This might be the perfect spot for Rick to recover.

He hurt like hell. He wanted to punch something—or maybe shoot at something—and then drink until he could fall to sleep without thoughts of her torturing his brain. He could do all of those things right here.

Chris handed Rick one of the glasses before he reached out and laid one hand on Darci's shoulder.

She'd stalked in from the kitchen, dishtowel still in hand, and was demanding answers.

"Give him a minute, darlin'," Chris said.

She glanced between Rick and her husband and then finally nodded.

Wow. Rick had always assumed no one would ever be able to silence his sister, but apparently Chris could. Miracles did happen.

Maybe there was hope for a miracle for him too.

Perhaps he would completely forget about Sierra Cox, aka Carey Jones, and be able to live a normal life again like he had been before her. B.C.—Before Carey.

"So the gun range just added late night hours seven days a week. We should go." Chris's suggestion, subtle but obvious at the same time, told Rick he was there for him whenever he needed.

For whatever he needed too, whether that was blowing holes in some paper targets at the range, or getting shit-faced on the bottle in front of them on the table.

"Yeah. That'd be good." Rick lifted the glass to his lips and let the whisky burn a path down to his fractured heart.

Friends, family and some fine whisky—it might take a while, but he'd be all right. Eventually.

The television was on, as was usual in Darci's house.

Some entertainment show was playing. One of those Hollywood-type programs that focused on movie stars and gossip.

He was used to tuning out the white noise of the television, but he'd had more than enough of Hollywood to last him a lifetime.

Rick didn't need the reminder following him home too. He stood to grab the remote on the other end of the table so he could change the channel, or at least mute the damn sound.

The remote was in his hand when he heard it. Her voice. Sierra.

She was standing outside in the sun, familiar sunglasses hiding her eyes as the show's host asked her questions about the film.

From his place in the chair, Chris mumbled the exact curse Rick had been thinking himself.

Fuck.

As his heart clenched and his stomach twisted, Rick eyed the bottle. He was going to need a bigger glass.

CHAPTER EIGHTEEN

Frowning, Jamey glanced at the deceivingly slim but fit guy dressed in black from head-to-toe as he stood in the hallway just outside the Green Room at the network's Time Square studio.

Sierra braced herself for the inevitable question.

"Where's Rick?" Jamey asked once they were both in the room alone and the bodyguard was outside the closed door.

She and Jamey had arrived in New York on different flights and this was the first time they'd been together since leaving Hollywood, so he wasn't aware of the change in her security detail . . . or her relationship status.

"He, uh, no longer handles my security."

Jamey's brows drew lower. He opened his mouth and then closed it again, visibly torn about what to say.

She decided to help him out. "Yes, we broke up."

He nodded. "You need to talk?"

"No." Talking was the last thing she needed.

In fact, if she could get out of doing this press tour and go hide in her house in Miami and not talk to anyone for the next two months or so, she'd would.

As it stood, her press obligations were clearly spelled out in her contract for this film, so she'd carry on.

Thank God she and Rick had never gone public with their relationship. Only a few people on set knew they'd dated or she'd have questions from every reporter she saw.

Lips pressed tight, Jamey gave the door that hid the bodyguard in the hall a quick glance. "He doesn't look like Rick."

Sierra couldn't help but laugh.

That had been her first thought too, right before she was grateful for that fact. She didn't need his doppelganger shadowing her as a reminder he was gone. She had the dull ache in her chest for that.

"Don't worry about me. I have it on good authority he's more than capable of handling any trouble," she assured Jamey.

She'd gotten that same assurance from Jon on

the phone, right before he'd told her that not all SEALs were as big as Rick.

Apparently Rick had handed filling her security needs over to his friend. Being Rick was always such a control freak about handling her security personally, she'd been surprised when Jon had contacted her.

Though maybe she shouldn't have been surprised. She'd said she wanted a clean break. Rick was giving her just that.

So why did she feel so disappointed when Jon's number kept appearing on her cell phone instead of Rick's?

Jamey was still quietly watching her. She could see his mind spinning with all the questions he was holding back.

"Do we have a script of what we're going to say about the Navy SEAL angle during the interviews?" Jamey finally asked. "They might show the footage from Coronado."

"They might. Or at least part of the scenes you shot on San Clemente Island. But why would we need a script?"

"What if they ask where we got two dozen Navy SEALs from?" Jamey asked, eyes wide.

She shrugged. "There's nothing to explain. We had a military contact who arranged it."

"Okay." He pressed his lips together again. Standing next to the juice and coffee set up in the room, he held a cup in his hand but didn't pour anything into it. "Um, can I ask you something?"

They might as well get this conversation over with since she could see he wasn't going to let it drop. "Sure."

"If I asked Rick to train me, do you think he'd agree? You know, like real Navy SEAL training. I'm reading some war movie scripts and trying to choose my next project."

She almost laughed at that. Of all the questions she'd been expecting, that was not one of them.

Relieved, she said, "I don't know. You could ask him."

Jamey wrinkled his nose. "One more question."

Sierra sighed. "Okay."

"Would that be a problem for you, if I brought him back out to LA?"

Her heart sped at the thought of being in the same city as Rick again. It seemed easier to be apart with a country between them, but if he was right there, just a cab ride away . . . How would she feel?

It didn't matter. They were done and it would be selfish of her to stop Rick from working wherever he wanted. She had to admit he was good on set, both as a consultant and on camera.

"No. No problem at all," she answered, hating how her pulse quickened at the idea of accidentally running into Rick again. "You should call him if that's what you want."

Jamey pressed his lips together, looking once again like he had something to say. Finally, he said, "I would, but I don't have his phone number."

She didn't know how Rick felt, but apparently the bromance between him and Jamey was still going strong as far as Jamey was concerned.

Squashing the envy that Jamey was going to get to talk to him, when Rick obviously didn't want to talk to her, she held out her hand. "Give me your cell. I'll put in his number for you."

One of Rick's security mandates had been that she had to memorize all important numbers and not depend on the saved contacts in her phone.

She still knew his number by heart, which meant it had done nothing when she'd deleted his name from her contacts list. She could still be tempted to call or text him in a moment of weakness . . . and there had definitely been weak moments the past couple of weeks.

And now she was giving Jamey the means to bring Rick back to Hollywood, right where she was going to be for the movie premiere, and for more press interviews and then when they started shooting the new film.

But she was probably being foolish even thinking there was a chance she could run into Rick again. He was probably already busy working for Jon. He could be overseas for all she knew.

Besides, there was no way Rick would come back to Hollywood. He hated it there.

Confident, she handed the cell back to Jamey. "Here you go."

"Thanks," he said, staring down the phone.

"No problem." Since he had yet to pour himself coffee, she moved between him and the coffee pot and got herself a cup.

Sleep had been hard for her lately and she felt it now as jet lag made the New York-based morning talk show feel even earlier.

"I'm sorry you broke up with him," Jamey said, glancing up at her. "You two were good together."

She lifted her brows. "How do you know I broke up with him and not the other way around?"

Jamey let out a sniff. "It was obvious he was head over heels for you."

Meaning it *wasn't* obvious that she loved him back? How could Jamey think that?

Of course, she had been the one who'd insisted they keep their relationship secret. But she'd let Rick go so he could be happy. She'd made that sacrifice for him because she cared about him.

Why didn't Jamey believe she had loved Rick as much as he loved her? She was about to ask when the door opened.

A young woman who had intern written all over her energetic face said, "You two are on next."

Jamey smiled at the girl. "Thanks." He turned and looked at Sierra. "Ready?"

Not at all. She'd never been less ready for a live interview in her life.

She drew in a breath and tossed the untouched coffee into the trash. Forcing a smile she didn't feel she said, "Ready."

CHAPTER NINETEEN

Deja vu was a horrible thing. It reminded Rick that he'd been here before. He'd taken a giant step backward in his life and landed right back where he'd started.

As Rick sat on the sofa, miserable, it could have easily been two years ago. Back when Chris and Darci had first started dating and he'd started to feel like an outsider in his own home. Then, and now, he sat in the living room and braced for when Chris and Darci would start knocking their headboard against the wall again.

Apparently marriage hadn't slowed down that activity any, as evidenced by what he'd heard last night from his bed.

Actually, he was worse off than he'd been back when he'd lived here. Then at least he'd had a good job at the nuclear reactor. He might have hated it, but at least he had it.

Yeah, he could ask Jon to assign him something, but he hadn't done it yet. He wasn't exactly sure why not, although he suspected he knew.

Somewhere inside him there was the hope that Sierra would change her mind. Come to her senses, call him and beg him to come back.

Hope sucked.

He needed to move on. He would. Eventually.

Glancing outside, Rick saw the sun had finally risen.

Why was he awake at the crack of dawn when his body should still be on California time and he had nothing else to do but sleep?

He knew the answer to that too.

It was because he'd never really gotten to sleep last night. Tossing and turning and watching the numbers change on the damn clock was an exercise in futility.

It was less frustrating to just get up. There was the ever present hope that television would distract him. Besides, the crack of dawn might be the only opportunity he'd get to control the remote.

Once Darci got up, she'd claim the remote and since this was technically her house and he hadn't lived or paid bills here for over two years, he wouldn't be able to argue.

The big screen on the wall came to life and an early morning talk show came one. He was about to surf the channels for something more interesting when the host said, "Next up, Sierra Cox and Jamey Garret."

Rick froze. He had the means to change the channel right in his hand. Unfortunately he didn't seem to have the will. Instead, he sat there through the commercial break, waiting.

Seeing her, hearing her, was going to hurt like hell.

He knew that yet he waited anyway, literally on the edge of his seat, leaning forward on the sofa cushion as if that would bring him closer to where she was in the studio in New York.

Pitiful.

Finally the commercial break ended and the show returned. With a burst of applause, Jamey and Sierra walked out, waving and holding hands.

Rick drew in a breath in an attempt to calm himself.

There's nothing going on between them.

As he watched, his gaze zeroed in on where Jamey touched Sierra, Rick repeated the sentence to himself over and over again.

Still, the doubts crept in.

Was that why she'd sent him away? Because she did have feelings for Jamey?

There was a lot of hugging and kissing as the two show hosts greeted the two movie stars.

Finally, they were all seated again and the interview began with the usual mundane questions.

What had the stars had been up to since arriving in New York? Did they get to take in any Broadway shows or try any restaurants? How were they handling the rainy weather in the city after being in the perfect weather of Los Angeles for so long filming?

A few of those questions cut Rick to the core. He and Sierra had planned on doing just that—seeing some shows and having dinner while in the city.

The only thing that made him feel moderately better was her saying that she'd arrived late the night before and hadn't seen anything except the limo and the hotel.

The show cut to commercial again, leaving him hanging.

His heart pounded as the minutes ticked by agonizingly slowly. Just when he thought he'd lose his mind if he saw one more ad, the show's music returned.

"Good morning," Darci's voice behind him had Rick waving one hand at her.

"Shh!" he said, without looking at her.

"What's—Oh." She came and sat next to him on the sofa, her eyes glued to the same thing Rick's were—Sierra.

"So, there were some pretty steamy love scenes between you two," one co-host said.

"Oh, yeah. The clip I saw was so hot I needed a

smoke after watching you two in bed," the other host agreed amid laughter from the audience.

Sierra smiled and shook her head. "That's all the magic of the movies. You wouldn't think it was so sexy if you were there on set."

"True," Jamey agreed. "Nothing like the director yelling *cut* because they could see my, uh, sock, if you know what I mean."

"I'm going to assume it's not a sock that's on your foot," one host said.

"You'd assume correctly." Sierra nodded with a smile.

"Let's take a look at that clip, shall we?" one host asked.

"I'm going to keep an eye out for that sock," the second host said, laughing.

The picture changed to the love scene Rick had spent too many hours watching during filming.

With the music added and the editing complete it looked completely different. He swallowed hard and consciously worked to keep the doubts from creeping back into his mind.

Sierra was either with Jamey now or she wasn't. It didn't matter because the end result was the same—she wasn't with Rick.

Oddly, that thought filled him with calm. Maybe because the thought of being left because she had feelings for another man would be easier to swallow than thinking he'd caused the break-up.

There was nothing he could do now or could

have done then to change her feelings if she'd fallen in love with Jamey.

It took the responsibility for the cause of the break-up off him if it hadn't happened because he'd fucked up or because he wasn't good enough for her. There would be something freeing in that.

There was one problem with his new theory, however. He didn't see any spark between the two stars in real life. Not in California when he'd been there with them and not now as they sat stiffly on camera next to each other and laughed at silly jokes.

Apparently, this movie was a huge deal, because the interview got not two, but three segments. The hosts threw to a commercial one more time with the promise they'd return and talk more with Sierra and Jamey.

Rick's torture wasn't over yet.

"You all right?" Darci asked.

"Yup. Just fine."

If she heard the lie in his voice she didn't say so. Instead, Darci stood and headed for the kitchen. "You make coffee yet?"

"Yes. When I got up."

"Good. I'll make breakfast. Pancakes and bacon good?" she asked.

"Perfect." Might as well eat his way through the heartache until it was a socially acceptable time to start drinking.

"And we're back with Jamey Garret and Sierra Cox. So, Jamey, you got to play a Navy SEAL in this movie."

"I did. And it was one of the most amazing experiences of my life."

"We've got a clip. Let's watch."

The Zodiac flashed onto the screen as it was tossed on the surf with Jamey aboard. The scene cut to the SEALs taking the beach and then the explosion.

Then Jamey was stretched out on the beach as the SEAL medic delivered his two lines, "*Look at me! Do not close your eyes, sailor.*"

Jamey did just that—closed his eyes and the scene ended.

"Wow. That was powerful," one host said.

"And you filmed with actual Navy SEALs as extras. What was that like?" the other host asked.

"It was amazing. Those guys," Jamey shook his head. "Let me tell you, I've never met such hard working, focused men in my life. And they are in amazing shape physically. We ran onto that beach dozens of times to get that one scene right. I was ready to drop right there and die every time the director called for another take, but they were all still laughing and joking. They'd just trot back out to the boat and do it all over again."

"I think we're all going to look forward to seeing what else you and the SEALs did when the movie opens next Friday night. Sierra, Jamey, thank you for coming to speak with us."

That was it. Rick got a glimpse of Sierra hugging the co-hosts and then there was another commercial filling the screen.

He drew in a breath. Okay, he'd survived that and now that it was over he could move on.

His cell phone was on the table where he'd tossed it when he'd crawled out of his room and threw himself on the sofa at dawn. He didn't know the number but he did recognize the area code. It was a Los Angeles number.

Was it Sierra calling from a different phone?

He dove for the cell and swiped the screen to answer the call. "Hello?"

"Rick, it's Jamey."

Not admitting the disappointment he felt, even to himself, Rick said, "Hey."

"Dude, did you see us on The Morning Show just now? I hope you saw it."

"Yeah, I saw it."

"That scene was pretty kick ass, right?"

He didn't need to ask which scene. He knew Jamey was all about the action—and not the action in bed with Sierra. "Yeah, it was pretty kick ass."

"So, I've been reading some scripts, looking for my next project and there are a couple of good ones. At least I think they're good."

"Okay." Where was this going? Rick had no clue.

Maybe Jamey just missed having a guy to talk to.

"Would you maybe take a look at the scripts for my top two choices and let me know what you think?"

"Me?" Rick asked. "I don't know anything about movie scripts."

"You know about the military though. These are both war movies."

Ah, things were beginning to become clear now.

The last thing he wanted to do was be involved in the movie business. It would only remind him of Sierra. But Jamey was a good kid, and it wasn't as if Rick had anything better going on at the moment.

"All right. Sure. Send them to me."

"Oh my God. That would be so great. Thanks."

Rick couldn't help but smile at Jamey's enthusiasm. "No problem."

There was dead air for a few second before Jamey said, "There's something else I wanted to ask you."

"Okay. Shoot."

"If either of these projects work out, would you consider letting me hire you? You know, to consult on the military stuff. Train me to get me into shape. Teach me about the weapons and maybe how to fight. It would probably only be three or four months you'd have to be in California and I'd pay you."

The dead last place Rick wanted to be right now was Hollywood. The place was packed full of memories and with memories came pain.

"Would a hundred-thousand dollar consulting

fee be enough?" Jamey asked. "I can give you more if you need. And I can rent you a place to stay while you're out there. Or you could stay with me at my place if you want."

Rick's eyes widened. This kid was the worst negotiator on earth, but a lot of things had come to light during this short conversation and that job offer.

First, there was no way Sierra and Jamey were together if the kid was inviting him to live with him. Second, earning a hundred thousand dollars just to tutor Jamey for a few months on how to not look like a civilian was insane.

"Um, can I think about it and get back to you?" Rick certainly had a lot to think about.

Judging by the speed with which Sierra had booked him a flight out, she didn't want him there in California. But who was to say she'd even be there? She could be in Miami or on location anywhere in the world.

He shouldn't turn down a good opportunity just on the off chance she might be there. And he really had enjoyed planning and shooting those scenes. He was good at it too—

"Oh, yeah. Sure. Of course," Jamey said, interrupting Rick's internal debate. "I mean I know you're probably busy. I just thought I'd ask and hope you'd consider it."

"I'll definitely consider it. Give me twenty-four hours. I'll call you with an answer. Thanks for thinking of me."

"Of course. So I, uh, will wait to hear from you

then."

"Yup. Bye." He disconnected the call and glanced up at his sister in the kitchen.

Darci had been joined by Chris, fresh from the shower judging by his wet hair.

Rick stood and walked to the kitchen island. Tossing his cell onto the countertop he said, "You're not going to believe what that was about."

CHAPTER TWENTY

Sierra adjusted her sunglasses as she slipped out of the back of the town car dropping her off in front of the hotel.

Today she'd get to sit in a room at the Beverly Hilton for eight hours while dozens of reporters funneled in one at a time and asked her the same questions over and over and over again. And she'd smile and answer every one of them as if she hadn't already done it twelve times already that day.

It was hellish but she'd get through it because finally she could see the light at the end of the tunnel. And Jamey would be there, enduring the hell with her, so that would help.

She just had to get through one more day and then she'd be done with her obligations for the movie that seemed to never end . . . unless it got award nominations.

Crap. If that happened then there'd be all the ceremonies to attend and countless more interviews.

It wasn't lost on her that at any other time in her life she'd be thrilled to think her movie could be up for awards.

How had things gotten turned so upside down? The little voice inside her whispered the answer to that question.

Rick.

She was so insane lately that she even imagined she saw him around town. Like right now, the guy across the street looked like him, walked like him.

Even sounded like him. It had been his laugh that had her looking up to begin with.

Wait . . . She narrowed her eyes and stared at the guy waiting on the other side of the street for the light to change.

It sure looked like him, but no. It couldn't be. Could it? He was in Virginia, wasn't he?

The Rick-lookalike belted out a deep belly laugh as the guy standing next to him said something. Then the light changed and the two started to cross the road.

They made it almost all the way across when the guy looked directly at her and stumbled to a halt. He stopped dead in the middle of the lane for a solid few seconds before he came to his senses and finished crossing the street.

On the curb, he said something to his friend and then turned to face where she stood.

There was no mistaking now. From this close up she was sure. It was Rick.

She remained right where she was, glued to the spot as he walked toward her.

"Hey," he said.

The sound of his voice cut right through her, making her want to sink to her knees as her shaky legs felt too weak to support her.

"Hi." Sierra noticed how breathy her voice sounded. "You look good."

"Do I?" He laughed.

"I didn't know you were back. What are you doing here?"

He snorted. "Don't worry. I'm not stalking you."

She shook her head. "I didn't think you were."

"I got offered a job out here," Rick continued, a lot colder than she imagined he'd be during all the times she'd considered how things would go if she should ever see him again.

She wanted to ask him where he was working and what he was doing but he'd glanced over his shoulder at the guy still standing just a few feet away waiting for him.

"Um, so I should go. It was good seeing you."

"You too."

For a second their gazes locked before, lips pressed tightly, he nodded and turned away from her to go and rejoin his friend.

When had Rick gotten friends in Hollywood? More, when had he gotten a job here?

None of that really mattered when there were so many other questions.

Why hadn't he hugged and kissed her hello? Asked if they could get together for a drink and to talk. Told her he still loved her and wanted them to be together again.

She feared she knew why. He'd gotten over her. Moved on.

Since this whole break up had been her idea, why hadn't she done the same?

Because she still loved him. Because breaking up had been a stupid misguided mistake.

And now it was too late.

On the verge of tears was not the place to be right now. She had to get to the makeup chair and then get her smiling self up to room eight-twelve and pretend she was happy to be there.

God, today was going to suck.

CHAPTER TWENTY-ONE

Rick walked into the dimly lit restaurant and headed directly for the bar. He ignored Jamey already seated there and instead said to the bartender, "Bourbon, straight up. Make it a double."

Jamey's eyes widened. "What happened?"

"Sierra Cox," Glen answered for Rick, and thank God for that because Rick wasn't sure he had it in him to explain at the moment.

Since Glen was the writer who was going to be reworking the script for the new movie Jamey had signed on to, he should have plenty of words at his disposal.

Right now, Rick didn't seem to have any.

"Damn. Sorry, man. But I guess it was bound to happen eventually. Hollywood's too small a town for you to have avoided her forever."

Rick spun to Jamey. "No, it's really not. Between residents and workers and tourists, it's a big fucking city."

Glen shook his head. "It might be a big city, but it's a small town when you're in our business."

Rick turned back and glanced down the bar. What was taking the bartender so long to pour a damn glass of bourbon?

Finally, he made his way from the other end and set the glass in front of Rick.

"Put that on my tab," Jamey said and then added, "and back him up with another one. Hell, make that three. One for each of us."

Rick let out a short laugh. It seemed Sierra Cox had the ability to drive everyone to drink.

"So what happened? What did she say?" Jamey asked.

"She wanted to know what I was doing here." Rick took a swallow and savored the burn.

Jamey frowned. "Damn. She wasn't a bitch to you, was she? That doesn't seem like her."

Dumping him out of the blue hadn't seemed like her either . . .

"She wasn't a bitch but she also didn't throw her arms around me and tell me she loves me either so . . ." Rick lifted a shoulder and reached for his glass again.

When he glanced back he saw Jamey watching

him.

"What?" Rick asked.

"I'm just wondering if you two just need to, you know, talk it out."

Rick let out a snort. "Nothing to talk about."

She'd dumped him in no uncertain terms. Booked him a flight and never bothered to call or text. Hell, they'd probably never have spoken again if he didn't happen to be crossing the street at the same time she was standing there.

"All right. If you say so. Anyway. Can I run over today's schedule with you?" Jamey asked.

Rick nodded. "Sure, shoot." Maybe work would distract him.

"From noon to eight p.m. I have those interviews at the Beverly Hilton."

Rick glanced at the time on his cell phone. "That's in an hour. You sure you should be drinking?"

Jamey blew out a breath. "Eight hours of what amounts to reporter speed-dating? Yeah, I'm gonna need more than one drink to get through that. But I figured you and Glen can work on the script together while I'm busy."

"Sure." Rick lifted a shoulder. "Whatever you want. I'm at your disposal."

For a hundred grand for twelve weeks work, plus living expenses, he could be accommodating.

"I'm glad you said that. I have a meal break

midway through. You think you could maybe meet me at the Hilton and just catch me up on what you two have been working on?"

"Okay."

"So say three o'clock? Room eight-twelve."

"But—" Glen began to say something.

Jamey's gaze cut to him. "Dude, I know you won't have a whole lot done by then, and it'll be rough, but I'd really like to see the two of you during my break. So three p.m. in room eight-twelve. Okay?"

Glen glanced from Jamey to Rick and back again. "Okay. If that's what you want."

Jamey nodded. "I think that's exactly what we need to do. A little meeting just to see how things stand."

Apparently Rick's new boss was real keen on having progress meetings. That was fine. He'd had worse bosses and done harder things for far less money. Bring it on.

Rick reached for his glass and took another sip. Piece of cake.

CHAPTER TWENTY-TWO

Time flies when you're having fun and though Rick would have never considered sitting in front of a stack of papers fun in the past, it had been today.

In the back booth of the restaurant with a mostly eaten burger on the table and the remains of a couple of bourbons, Rick leaned back and surveyed what they'd accomplished.

He glanced up at Glen. "So I need you to tell me because I don't know. Are we doing good here?"

Glen's eyes widened behind his wire framed glasses. "We're doing great."

"Really?" Rick asked.

He straightened the stack of pages he'd pulled out of the binder by tapping them on end against the table. When the papers weren't strewn all over, it didn't seem like a whole lot. They still had so much more to go.

"Trust me. We're kicking ass on this."

"Okay. If you say so." Rick glanced at his cell. "It's fourteen-forty-five. We'd better head over to the hotel."

"Mmm-hmm." Glen shoved his glasses up his nose and got busy putting things into his big leather bag. Suddenly in a rush, he stood. "Ready to go?"

Rick frowned. "Do you need to sign something here?"

"Shit. Yeah. Let me just go close out Jamey's tab. Be right back." He turned to go then looked back. "Don't go anywhere."

"I'm not moving a muscle." Rick laughed.

This guy sure was nervous.

Though he supposed if it were his words he'd be showing to his boss, he might be too. Luckily he was just a consultant, not a writer.

"Okay. Ready. Let's go." After a glance back, Glen power-walked out the door and across the street.

Rick followed, taking one long stride to every two of Glen's shorter ones as he wondered what he was so nervous about since they had plenty of time to get across the street to the hotel.

The man must have been really nervous about

what Jamey would think of the work they'd done. He didn't say a word on the walk over, or in the elevator ride up.

In fact, it wasn't until they stood in front of the room door that Rick finally decided he needed to break the silence.

He laid one hand on Glen's shoulder. He jumped beneath Rick's touch.

"Dude. Relax. If he doesn't like what we did, we'll do it over. No big deal."

Pale, Glen stared wide-eyed at Rick. Finally, he said, "Okay." Then he knocked on the door and took one big step backward.

Hollywood people were strange.

Frowning, Rick glanced back at him and then turned and waited for the door to open. It took a while but finally the door swung wide and Jamey stood there.

"Good. You're here," Jamey said.

"Yup." Rick hooked a thumb back at Glen. "We've got some pages to show you but it's all just preliminary."

"That's fine. Come on in." Jamey backed up and motioned for Rick to come inside. "Why don't you go on into the other room and I'll meet you in there."

"Why are you whispering?" Rick said, keeping his own voice down too.

"There's, um, uh, interviews happening in the

room next door. Microphones are sensitive."

"Oh. Okay." Rick nodded and tried to walk more softly than usual as he made his way past the sofa and table to the door of the other room in the suite.

Opening it, he found the room empty of people but not of stuff.

They'd obviously used this portion of the suite as a staging area. Make-up, bags, clothes, snacks and drinks littered every flat surface.

It would be easier to work on the script out in the other room on the table.

Rick couldn't figure out why Jamey had suggested he come in here. Then the bathroom door swung open and Rick knew exactly why he was in this room.

"Sierra." He shouldn't be surprised.

Now all the strangeness between Jamey and Glen made sense.

"Rick." Her mouth dropped open. "What are you doing here?"

He shook his head. "Getting tricked, I believe."

"I'm sorry, but you two need to talk." Jamey's voice came through the door.

Drawing in a breath, Rick turned toward the door and tried to open it. Something was preventing him from turning the knob. "Are you holding the doorknob?"

"Yes," Jamey said.

Rick lifted a brow. "You do know I can get this door open if I really want to, right?"

"Yes. And you can also kill me with your bare hands. But I'm betting that you won't do either."

The kid was right. He wouldn't.

Sighing, Rick turned to Sierra. "I guess we're in here for a little while."

"Rick, you have to believe I had nothing to do with this."

"I know." Rick was sure she didn't want to be in here with him any more than he wanted to be there with her. He tipped his head. "You look good too. I should have told you that when I saw you before on the street."

He'd been too shocked, mostly by how much it hurt to see her again.

Sierra's eyes drifted closed, before she opened them again. "I don't feel good. I haven't been able to move on. At least not as well as you have."

"You think I've moved on?" He let out a bitter laugh. "Not even close, princess. Not even close."

"I'm so, so sorry." She shook her head as her eyes began to look glassy.

"So am I." His fists clenched at his sides, it took all his will power not to reach for her.

The first tear cascaded down her cheek and his control broke.

With a curse, he closed the distance between

them with a few steps, pulled her against him and held her close.

"I still love you. And I hurt so bad." Her voice was muffled from his palm pressing her head against his chest.

He dropped his hand to her shoulder and pulled back so he could see her face when he said, "Me too."

There was a glimmer of hope in her tear-filled eyes, even as her lip quivered.

Her tears always did have the power to break him. And damn it felt so good to have her in his arms again.

It might turn out to be the worst decision of his life but he couldn't stop himself and he didn't want to. He leaned down and pressed his lips to hers. Softly. Gently.

She gasped and kissed him back.

That was all it took. The kiss went from zero-to-sixty in seconds.

Before he knew it he had her pinned against the wall.

He held her hands above her head as he shoved his thigh between hers.

She pressed against him, riding his leg and whimpering from the friction.

His tongue plunged against hers as he tried to calculate how far the bed behind them was. Too far, he decided as he shoved the tote bag off the dresser next to them, hoisted her up and planted her on top.

"I love you," Rick said between kisses.

"I love you," she replied.

"Want you. Need you." Hand tangled in her hair, Rick moved down to bite her neck and felt the resulting tremor run through her. She always did have a sensitive throat.

"I hated being apart from you," she said, sounding breathless.

"Me too. Every fucking second."

She pulled away to look at him. "I was stupid. I don't know what I was thinking. Can you forgive me?"

"Yes." He drew in a breath and captured her face between his palms. "But don't ever do anything like that again."

"I won't. I promise." She shook her head.

He wiped the new tears from her eyes before moving in on her lips.

Rick bent over her, but couldn't seem to get close enough. He raised one knee on top of the dresser, bending Sierra back beneath him as she wrapped her arms around his neck.

Something fell and hit the ground with a smash. He ignored the sound and kept kissing her.

He didn't care about anything until he heard the click of the door.

Breaking the kiss, he tipped his head to glance at the doorway. He found Jamey standing there next to Glen.

Grinning, Jamey elbowed Glen. "Now that's what a love scene is supposed to be like."

Shaking his head at Jamey's comment, Rick straightened up, pulling Sierra upright with him.

"He's right, you know." Sierra smiled.

"I know. Let's not tell him. It'll go to his head."

She peeked at Jamey past Rick and said, "I think it already has."

Rick found himself unable to control a smile that was almost as big as Jamey's. "Eh, that's okay. I guess we can let him have his victory this once."

The kid deserved it. It was his trickery that had gotten them back together.

Who knew how long it would have taken them to straighten things out on their own, if it would have ever happened at all. That was too horrifying to consider.

Rick ignored the audience and leaned low to press another kiss to Sierra's lips to remind himself of what he'd missed and what he'd never do without again. No matter what.

EPILOGUE

"Again? Really?" Sierra asked, glancing up from the cup of coffee she'd been longingly looking forward to. "I thought we nailed it that time."

The assistant director lifted one shoulder. "Jim wants just one more take."

Sierra sighed. "All right."

She really shouldn't complain. This shoot had gone smoothly so far. If an extra take was the biggest thing she had to deal with on this film she'd consider herself lucky.

It had been the right thing to do, taking this movie. The public had yet to weigh in with their box office dollars, but in her gut she felt it. It was good. They'd love it.

And if they didn't?

Maybe that didn't matter that much. She'd made this one for herself. If it bombed, at least she knew she'd done her best with a project she'd chosen.

Sierra moved back to her mark—standing in front of her dressing table and looking at herself in the mirror.

At this point in the story the character is starting to wonder if she'd lost her mind or if there really was someone or something following her.

In this shot, she hears something and startles, but it turns out to be just her friend coming to check on her.

The scene was fairly simple, which is why it didn't make a whole lot of sense the director wanted another take. But whatever the director wanted, the director got.

"And action!"

Sierra cleared her expression and waited for her cue to react. Except the cue didn't come.

Instead, motion behind her reflected in the mirror caught her attention.

In the reflection she saw Rick move closer.

"Rick?" She spun to face him. "What are you doing?"

She glanced around and saw the crew gathered around. Half were smiling. The other half looked shocked.

"What did you do?" she asked him, although it was becoming obvious as he dropped to one knee.

She pressed a hand to her mouth and sucked in a breath.

"Sierra . . . Carey, will you marry me?" he said as he held up the tiny box containing a ring.

She didn't seem to have words so she nodded instead. Nodded hard and fast until the tears filled her eyes even as she smiled.

Rick stood to slip the ring on her finger as everyone on the set broke into applause.

"And cut!" Jim yelled and stood.

Rick turned as the director neared. "Thanks for this, Jim."

"Are you kidding. I'm totally using that footage for the publicity tour. So thank you. The public will eat this up."

Sierra laughed and looked at Rick. "I can't believe you did this."

"It's kind of perfect, right?" he asked, smiling.

"Yes. And you're kind of perfect too."

Taking both her hands in his, Rick said, "We're perfect together."

"Yeah, we are."

"This totally should be a movie. We could call it 'The Bodyguard and the Star'," one PA suggested.

"Or wait, how about this? 'A SEAL in Hollywood'," another said. "You know, because he just did that SEAL movie with Jamey Garret."

Sierra listened to the chatter around them and caught Rick's eye. "You okay with our life being like this? Public?"

He took a step closer and leaned low. "As long as I can live it with you, I wouldn't have it any other way."

Read how Rick & Sierra's romance began in
Protected by a SEAL

Hot SEALs

For more titles by Cat visit CatJohnson.net

ABOUT THE AUTHOR

Cat Johnson is a top 10 *New York Times* bestseller and the author of the *USA Today* bestselling Hot SEALs series. She writes contemporary romance featuring sexy alpha heroes and is known for her unique marketing. She has sponsored pro bull riders, owns a collection of camouflage and western wear for book signings, and has used bologna to promote romance novels.

Never miss a new release or a deal again. Join Cat's inner circle at catjohnson.net/news for email alerts.

Made in the USA
San Bernardino, CA
26 November 2018